BELLA'S COWBOY DADDY

Rescue Ranch Book Four

MELINDA BARRON

Published by Blushing Books
An Imprint of
ABCD Graphics and Design, Inc.
A Virginia Corporation
977 Seminole Trail #233
Charlottesville, VA 22901

Melinda Barron
Bella's Cowboy Daddy

eBook ISBN: 978-1-64563-937-4
Print ISBN: 978-1-64563-938-1
v1

Prologue

Bella's Musings
By Bella Beaumont
© The Bookman Gazette

Keeping a secret in a small town is virtually impossible. It's not as if those words are a surprise to anyone. If your neighbors have overnight guests, you know it. If your co-worker is having an affair, you know it. If your friend's son is involved in something illegal, you know it.

Or at least you think you do. Sometimes the things you think are true turn out to be lies and sometimes things are buried, buried so deeply you don't really learn about them until someone is dead.

That is the case with me. I thought I knew my father, inside and out. He was a good man. A teacher. A coach. An animal lover who rescued strays. A newspaper publisher. A good husband. A wonderful father. A fantastic friend.

But after my father's recent death I found out he also kept a secret, one that affected Bookman Springs for fourteen years, and continues to cast a shadow over our town. Everyone who lives in Bookman Springs knows the story. Fourteen years ago, a person, or persons unknown, broke into the museum and took Native American artifacts: pottery, a box of arrowheads, and a spear.

Last week those items were found. How they were found is what is of importance to me. It seems my father held the secret all these years. According to information he left in his will, he found out a few of his students were involved in the theft. To keep them from getting into trouble he took the artifacts from them and buried them out in the country.

Why did he do it this way? I can't tell you, because the only thing he said was he wanted to keep them from getting into trouble. Dad made sure the items were recovered, but he did not name the thieves. He took that secret to his grave.

I've had a great many of our neighbors ask about the situation. All I can tell you is to read the news story on the first page. I don't know who took the items, and I doubt we will ever find out.

But there is one thing I do know. Now is the time to put the incident to rest. It is time to move on. It is time to heal.

On behalf of my mother and my brothers I am authorized to apologize to the citizens of Bookman Springs. Not for the theft, but for the cover up. We are happy the items are back with the tribe, and are sorry it took so long. We can give no excuses for why Dad did the things he did. But we are happy they have been found.

Chapter 1

Bella Beaumont took a step back as the doorway to Rowdy's opened before she could grab the handle. A cloud of cigarette smoke followed the cowboy who walked out the door. Loud country music followed in his wake. He saw her standing there, tipped his hat in her direction and held the door open and said, "Ma'am."

Even at thirty-four years of age she wasn't used to men in their early twenties calling her ma'am. She felt so old right now.

"Thanks," she said as she entered the bar. She didn't want to be here. After an eight-year hiatus from Wyatt Coleman's company she'd been thrown into the same room as him too many times in the last few weeks; and now here she was, about to initiate another conversation. With what she had in her pocket, this meeting could be one of many. She wasn't sure how she felt about that.

Getting over Wyatt Coleman had not been easy. She was eighteen and he was sixteen when they started their thing. It had ended when she was twenty-six, and there were times when he, both as a Dom and as her Daddy, still fueled her fantasies. The fact he was a man who couldn't keep it in his pants was what had ended their relationship.

Wyatt was a ho-dog, which was in direct contrast with his ability to treat a woman like a lady. Years ago, when they had lost their virginities to each other, he'd kept her secret, despite the fact it made him the main suspect in an infamous theft of Native American relics that still haunted the town of Bookman Springs, Texas.

The relics had been recovered by Wyatt's brother Reed, and his wife of one-week Leslie. Much to Bella's chagrin it had been a video from her late father that had uncovered the items. But her father had not revealed who had stolen the relics, only that he'd taken them and hidden them to keep the person—or persons responsible from getting into trouble. The small town's rumor mill had gone into overdrive, and it had centered on Wyatt Coleman, a known troublemaker.

But the night the theft had occurred from the museum, Wyatt had been taking her virginity. Over the years she'd told him she was going to let everyone know there was no way he was the thief, but Wyatt would not let her. He'd even gone so far as to tell her that he would denounce her words and say she was lying just to protect him.

"Your reputation is more important than mine," he'd said over and over.

So she'd let it pass, and the rumors had died down. Until now. Now that the relics had been recovered, and given back to the tribe, people were once again besmirching Wyatt's name and saying he'd done the deed. Now they were saying she knew and was covering it up in the newspaper she ran.

And then there was the letter, a copy of which she had in her pocket right now. Her hands shook as she thought about it. She'd received many complaints from people over the years, but she'd never had a death threat before. There was a part of her that wondered if she shouldn't go see Hawk, Wyatt's brother and the town constable, and show it to him instead of Wyatt. There was no telling what Wyatt would do with the information.

Wyatt was a hothead, and could fly off the handle at a moment's notice. The letter might send him into overdrive, which wouldn't be a good thing.

Bella made her way to the bar and stopped at the end. She surveyed the crowd. The pool tables and the dance floor were crowded, and there was every chance Wyatt was in one of those places, since she didn't see him sitting at the bar, or at any of the tables.

"Bella Beaumont!"

She turned her attention to the bartender who had just called out her name.

"Bert Lynch," she responded. "I haven't seen you in a month of Sundays. How are you?"

She'd graduated with Bert. He was now the owner of Rowdy's, which he'd named because of his youth, when he'd been a troublemaker, just like Wyatt.

Bert swept his arm out and said, "Busy and making money, which is a good thing. Can I get you a beer? First one's on the house for you."

"Sounds good," she said. She reached into her pocket for a tip, and watched as Bert made his way to the cooler where he pulled out a Mexican imported beer and twisted off the top.

He approached her and said, "If I remember correctly you're an out of the bottle drinker."

"No need to dirty a glass," she said as he set the bottle in front of her. Bella took a generous swig, then said, "I'm looking for Wyatt."

"Really?" Bert's eyes widened. "I thought the two of you avoided each other at all costs."

"I need to discuss something with him," she said. The piece of paper in her pocket felt warm, as if it would catch on fire. She had to share it with someone, and since it was about her, and Wyatt, he seemed the logical choice. But once again she wondered if she should call Hawk instead. She shook her head. Best to keep it between herself and her former lover.

"There's a couple of tables on the other side of the dance floor," Bert said. "He's usually sitting over there with his flavor of the night."

"Thanks." She picked up her beer and started in the direction Bert had indicated. As she made her way there she nodded at people who called her name in greeting, but didn't stop to talk. She wanted to get this over with.

She spotted Wyatt sitting in a corner. His cowboy hat was tipped back, and there was a blonde woman sitting next him, her hand in Wyatt's lap. His eyes were closed and there was, what her father always called, a shit-eating grin on his face. The woman's movements told Bella what was happening. She was jacking Wyatt off. If there was one thing Wyatt loved it was sex in public.

Memories flooded her brain—of the time he'd fucked her behind the newspaper office at the Fourth of July town gathering; of the time he'd fingered her at the movie theater and she'd had to bite her hand to keep from screaming out his name when she came; and of the time he'd fucked her at the county rodeo, eating her out first while two old cowboys talked about horses not twenty feet away. Minutes later she'd had to participate in the barrel racing competition, the memory of Wyatt's cock thrusting inside her pushing her to finish first. He'd made her wear the sash she won, and only the sash, to bed that night.

Thinking about it made her pussy wet. She glanced to where Wyatt sat, and to her surprise his eyes were no longer closed. He was looking directly at her, and his smug smile was still prevalent.

"Hello darlin'," he called out, his voice rising above the music. "Come and visit."

Bella fought the urge to turn tail and run. She patted the letter in her pocket and knew she needed to do what was necessary.

She made her way to the table, and as she walked she saw several people whispering behind their hands. It would be all over town by Monday that Bella had gone hunting for Wyatt on Saturday night. Were they getting back together? Or was she looking for a booty call?

When she was at the table she set down her beer.

"I need to talk to you," she said.

"So talk," Wyatt responded.

To her surprise he pushed the blonde's hand away from his lap.

"Hey," the woman said.

Not to her surprise, Wyatt's hands went to his lap, and from their movement, Bella was sure he was zipping up his pants. Some things never changed.

"We need to talk," she said.

"You pregnant?" he asked, and then he laughed. "Sweetie, I'm sure my boys are good swimmers, but they're not that good. It's been a while."

Bella took a deep breath. "Wyatt, I'm serious. Something has come up that I need to talk to you about."

"On a Saturday night?" he asked. He leaned over and kissed the blonde on the shoulder. "Give me a few minutes, sweetie."

Every woman was sweetie, or darlin' to him, Bella thought.

"But I thought we were going to fuck," the woman asked, her words slightly slurred.

"Later," Wyatt answered.

"Tell the bitch to go away," the blonde said. Then she batted her eyes at Wyatt.

"Behave, and give me some time, or you'll spend the night by yourself," Wyatt said.

The woman pushed back from the table. She stood and stalked toward the main part of the bar. When she passed Bella she threw her hand out, and slapped Bella in the shoulder. In her younger years, Bella would have tackled the woman and started a catfight. But she was the publisher of the paper now, and she had a reputation to uphold.

"Behave!" Wyatt called out. When the flavor of the night was gone, Wyatt glanced up at her. "Want to finish what she started?"

"Fuck you, Wyatt," Bella said. She'd had the whole thing planned, how she was going to calmly tell Wyatt about the letter, and ask him what he thought they should do. But his attitude pissed her off.

"We can always fuck in the bathroom, but you know... gross." He winked at her, and her anger intensified. "Of course there is my truck outside. I seem to remember you never minded being bent over the hood. A few good swats and you'll be wetter than a sidewalk in a hurricane."

She was always wet, but there was no way she was going to tell him that. If she stood here much longer there was every chance she would take him up on his offer. He might fuck every weekend but it had been a year since she'd had a dick inside her, and Wyatt's cock was the best she'd ever had.

"Screw you!"

"That's the idea," Wyatt said. "If you prefer we can use that fancy car of yours. I'm sure the seats fold down and being inside it would give us a little more privacy. Not that discretion ever mattered to you."

That was it. She couldn't stand here and take anymore from him. Bella pulled the letter from her pocket and tossed it on the table. "Read it for yourself, and then go to hell."

Bella stalked off through the people who had gathered to

watch. She waited to hear Wyatt call out or tell her to come back, but nothing came. People on the dance floor had stopped moving and were staring at her as she moved to the front door. The door opened just as it had when she'd come in; she sailed through it and went to her SUV, her hands shaking as she climbed behind the wheel.

Damn she hated that man. She hated the way he made her feel, and the fact she wanted to do as he'd suggested. She wanted to sit down at the table and jerk him off, or better yet go down on him. The fact that her pussy was wet made her even madder. All these years later and he still made her so damn horny she thought she would go crazy.

She pressed the button to start her car and then put it in gear. She'd parked so she didn't have to back up, but when she hit the gas she immediately slammed on the brake as Wyatt appeared in front of her.

He was holding the letter, clutched in his hand and yelled, "What the fuck is this?"

"Looks like a death threat," Bella screamed in return. "Good luck figuring out where it came from. Now get the hell out of my way."

Wyatt planted his hands on the hood of Bella's fancy SUV, the piece of paper hot in his hands. "Turn off the engine."

In response she gunned it, but it was obvious she had her foot on the brake, too, because the car barely moved. Either that or she'd put it in park and he hadn't noticed. "Get out of the car."

From behind him, Wyatt heard laughter. He turned to see a crowd of bar-goers gathered to watch the confrontation. Damn, this was all he needed. Since the retrieval of the artifacts, people had been talking about him behind his back and turning away from him when they saw him in town.

The word used most often, he knew, was thief. The widespread thoughts in Bookman Springs was that he'd taken the Indian artifacts and his brother had found them hidden not out in the boonies where it had been reported, but buried on the Rescue Ranch. The lie, people thought, was an effort to save Wyatt's reputation and keep him from possibly being charged in the theft.

If those stupid people did any research they would know the statute of limitations on theft was way past, and even if he had stolen the objects he couldn't be charged.

"Move out of my way!" Bella yelled from inside the car.

He shook the paper at her again. "Tell me what this is, and where you got it."

Bella gunned the motor again.

"Run me over if you have to!" Wyatt pointed behind her. "Either that or hit the car that's parked there. Either way you'll be up the proverbial creek."

"I hate you, you fucker!" she screamed.

The gathering crowd broke out in laughter.

Wyatt turned to them and shouted, "Get lost."

"Not a chance in hell," a male voice called out.

Wyatt knew if he stepped out from in front of the vehicle, Bella would take off, and he'd end up running to his truck and following her to her house. He couldn't decide if that was the best way to handle things, or if he should think of something else.

He stared through the windshield and saw her glaring back at him. Damn she looked sexy sitting there, her anger rolling off her. They'd always had their best sex when one of them was angry.

"Move!" Bella slammed her hands against the steering wheel.

Wyatt moved his hands from the hood, then moved to the side. Before she could put the car in gear he climbed on top of the car, his back against the windshield. He'd effectively blocked her view. Then he pulled his phone from his pocket and sent a text to Hawk. Sometimes it helped to have a brother who was in law enforcement.

Meet me at the ranch, ASAP, he texted.

There was a pause, and then Hawk's response came: *You kill someone?*

Not yet, Wyatt replied. *But if I don't show up within twenty minutes there is every chance Bella might have run me over.*

Again? Hawk texted.

Wyatt put his phone away. He settled against the windshield and called out, "Someone get me a rope."

The SUV moved, as he had expected. A cowboy he didn't know ran up and handed him a rope.

"Already tied in a lasso," the young man said, and Wyatt knew he would be telling his friends this story for years to come.

"Thanks," Wyatt said. He slid off the hood and banged his fist against the hood. Pain shot up his arm, but he ignored it. He fell to his knees and called out, "You hit me! You hit me!"

Bella was out of the car in seconds, her hands in fists. He jumped up and grinned. "Gotcha."

She slammed a fist into his chest, but before she could hit him again he took a step back, threw the rope around her and tightened the lasso.

"You son of a bitch!" she called out as he lowered his shoulder and threw her over it. She kicked at him but her hands were effectively out of commission.

Wyatt crossed to the back of the SUV and lifted the hatch. He tossed Bella inside, then used the last of the rope to hogtie her.

"I'll get you for this!" she yelled. "I swear you'll be in jail!"

"It wouldn't be the first time," he said with a chuckle.

After he'd lowered the hatch he went to the front of the vehicle. "Show's over," he called out. He got behind the wheel of the car and put it in gear. As he pulled out of the parking lot, Bella continued to scream and call him names.

Damn he'd missed this woman. The only problem with tying her up right now was he would not be able to fuck her afterward.

Or maybe he would. This sort of thing always got her motor running. Maybe he would be able to talk her into a little extra kidnapping activity. Something told him it would be one of their best fucks ever.

Chapter 2

"I want him in handcuffs!" Bella's body shook as the vehicle hatch opened and she saw Wyatt and Hawk looking down at her. "He kidnapped me!"

How in the hell had she fallen for his trick? Was she that out of practice in dealing with Wyatt? She should have known she hadn't hit him, because the car had not been moving.

"Shit, Wyatt," Hawk said. "What were you thinking?"

"She was going to run me over," Wyatt said. "I was protecting myself. There's a whole score of witnesses back at the bar."

"Drunken witnesses," Hawk said.

Wyatt leaned over and loosened the ropes around her ankles. When they were free she kicked out at him.

"Watch it," Wyatt said, although he sounded more amused than annoyed. "You almost got the family jewels."

He lifted her onto her feet and she wiggled to try and get away from the rope that was still wrapped around the upper portion of her body. "I'm serious, Hawk, I want him arrested. I'm filing charges."

"Will you just calm down," Wyatt said.

"Calm down?" The rope fell to the ground and she started to swing at him. He turned her so her back was to him and grabbed her tightly, holding her so her back was to his chest.

"Stop," Wyatt said.

She hated the thought he was laughing at this situation, and all the Coleman brothers, and their wives, were watching. She saw Holt and his wife, Aurora, on the porch. Aurora had little Amelia Grace, a little more than a week old in her arms. Jessica, Hawk's wife, stood next to her. The other woman was Lizbeth, Austin's girlfriend. Austin, the youngest Coleman, and Kyle, stood nearby and she wondered if they were ready to jump in if a true fight broke out between herself and Wyatt. The only one of the Coleman brothers missing was the newly married Reed and his wife Leslie. They were still on their honeymoon in Las Vegas.

Reed, Kyle and Wyatt were triplets, and Bella had often wondered how the three of them were so different since they'd shared a womb for nine months.

"You bastard," she growled at Wyatt.

"I assure you, my parents were married," Wyatt said.

"You're the feral one of the bunch," Bella said. "I'm sure you snuck in somehow since you're the ass of the family."

"You used to like my ass," Wyatt said, and then he burst into laughter.

Bella launched herself at him. She slapped him as hard as she could, and then someone—Hawk? Kyle? Austin?—grabbed her.

"Enough!" Hawk's commanding voice filled the air. "I'll take the both of you to jail if someone doesn't tell me what the hell is going on here."

Wyatt dug in his pocket and thrust the letter in Hawk's direction. Bella hated that letter. She was so pissed at herself for taking it to Wyatt tonight instead of waiting until Monday and bringing it out to the ranch. Or even mailing it to him.

But the words had shaken her so much she'd had to share it with someone, and since it was about her, and Wyatt, he seemed the logical choice.

"What is this?" Hawk asked.

"It's a death threat," Wyatt said. "Someone wants to kill me, and Bella."

Hawk unfolded the paper. Holt came up and said, "Let's go inside and keep this private, please."

What was that supposed to mean, Bella wondered. There was nobody on the ranch but them, and the horses the men rescued and took care of before they adopted them out. She didn't think the horses would be telling anyone about this situation.

She didn't question his words, though, and when Holt held out his hand to indicate she should go first she started toward the ranch house. She heard the rattle of paper and imagined Hawk trying to read the letter in the moonlight.

When they were all in the house, Austin stepped forward. He pointed a finger at Bella. "Sweet tea? Or beer? Or a glass of wine?"

"She prefers whiskey, the good stuff," Wyatt said. "Or imported beer, no glass."

Bella sneered at Wyatt, then said, "The tea, please, Austin. Thank you."

"Got it," Austin said. He headed toward the kitchen and Jessica fell into step behind him.

"Let's go in the den," Holt said. "That's where we were, watching a movie. There's lots of food up there, and we can talk."

Bella looked to where Hawk stood near the door. He was reading the letter, and she saw the deep frown on his face. When he was done he let his hand fall to his side and said, "Son of a bitch. I thought this was over."

"So did I," Bella said. She mentally yelled at her late

father, and the situation he'd left for Reed, the absent brother, to find Indian artifacts that had been stolen from the museum fourteen years ago. Reed and Leslie had found them, and they'd returned the items to the tribe. But they'd never found out who had stolen them. Truthfully, they hadn't even tried. It was enough for Reed that he'd done his part.

But it was obvious from the letter that the thief—or thieves —were still in town and they didn't want to be found out.

Those people also thought Wyatt, and Bella, knew who they were.

"Upstairs," Holt said. "Bella, you know where it's at."

Yes, she did. She'd been in this house many times. She'd snuck in while the whole family was here so she and Wyatt could make good use of his bed. Now was not the time to think about it, though. She started toward the stairs on the far side of the room. As she climbed the Colemans fell into step behind her. She turned her head enough to see Wyatt was the first one on the stairs.

Once she was in the den she thought Holt's pronounce- ment about food was an understatement. There was a table set up near the wall with what looked like a buffet, which included two slow cookers, a plate of bread, another plate of cold cuts, and a basket of fruit.

"Just some movie snacks," Austin said as he came up beside her. He handed her a large glass of tea and she took a swig, savoring the sweetness.

"Thanks," Bella said. She felt much calmer now.

"Help yourself," Austin said.

"Thanks, but I'm not really hungry," she said. The people who had been here before were sitting down, and Bella saw a loveseat that was unoccupied. There was a basinet near Aurora, and Holt sat next to her. There were also trays near the occupants with half-eaten plates of food, and she wondered how much Austin and his lady friend had cooked that night.

Bella sat down, and to her chagrin Wyatt sat down next to her. She pulled her thigh away from him, and would have found another place to sit, but the room was full.

"Who wants to fill us in?" Hawk asked once he was seated.

"I think the letter speaks for itself," Bella said.

"Can pieces of paper talk?" Wyatt asked.

"Don't be a smart ass," Bella responded. She waved a finger at Hawk. "Read it."

Hawk held up the paper and said, *"You think you're so smart. But giving away my stuff was a mistake. I've waited a long time for it. The pictures in the paper didn't show it all, did they? You have it. It's mine. Give it back. Tell anyone about me and the two of you are dead. You have until Friday night."* Hawk lowered the paper. "You have what? And this was addressed to the two of you?"

"It was sent to me, at my house, in a manila envelope," Bella said. "The white envelope inside it was addressed to me and Wyatt."

"Where is it?" Hawk asked.

"At my house," she said. "I made a copy of the letter and put the original and the envelopes in my safe. Then I went in search of jerk-off here." Bella pointed at Wyatt.

"You say the most wonderful things to me," Wyatt said. He puckered his lips and made kissy noises.

"Wyatt, knock it off," Hawk said.

"Oh, I love you, too." Wyatt blew kisses in his brother's direction.

"Still haven't grown up," Bella said.

"You thought I was a grown up when we were having sex," Wyatt said.

"Wyatt!" This came from Holt. "Show some respect."

Bella turned her gaze on Wyatt, who actually looked abashed.

"My apologies, Bella," he said.

She knew the next part would be her saying something to accept his apology. She cleared her throat and said, "Okay." It wasn't much, but she couldn't bring herself to say she accepted his words.

The urge to run was strong, but Bella stayed where she was. "There's only one problem with the Friday deadline," she said. "Today is Saturday, and I have no idea how long that letter has been sitting in my pile of mail. They could mean Friday as in yesterday. I generally open my mail on Saturday nights."

"Exciting," Wyatt said.

He was right there. She could jam her elbow into his side and be gratified if he cried out in pain. Do it, do it, do it! One part of her cried out. The other part told her to behave. Before she could do anything Hawk spoke up.

"If that was so there's every chance you would have come to harm today." The lawman leaned forward with his elbows on his knees. "I need the original so I can see if there are prints on it. Did it come in the mail? Or was it delivered to the newspaper? You live above it, right?"

Bella nodded. "Everything is delivered to the office, and if it's addressed to me and obviously personal I take it upstairs, where it piles up until Saturday."

"Do you have a glass of wine while you open your mail? Or is that too much fun?"

This time she didn't resist. She slammed her elbow into Wyatt's side.

"Oh fuck," Wyatt said, and then to her surprise he laughed. "About time you showed some spunk."

"Spunk? This coming from the man who kidnapped me?" She pointed her finger at Hawk. "I want him arrested."

Hawk shook his head. "Are you going to cover the arrest

for the newspaper? Or will you let one of the reporters write the story about how he hogtied you?"

"Half the bar was watching, so the whole town will know by tomorrow morning," Bella said. Even as the words left her mouth the reality of it sunk in; it was one thing for drunks to spread the rumors, but it was another for people to read about it in the weekly paper.

"Fine." Hawk stood. "I'm off duty so I don't have cuffs. I'll go to the truck and get them."

"Stop," Bella called out before Hawk could leave the room. Then she turned to Wyatt. "You're an ass."

"Stop the presses!" Wyatt said, and then he laughed. "But of course that's not news to anyone, and printing it won't sell any newspapers. The whole town thinks I'm an ass."

"The whole town is right," she muttered.

"It's late on a Saturday night," Hawk said. "I'll come by for the letter in the morning. In the meantime, I think you should stay here at the ranch, just in case."

"I'm not hiding." Bella stood. "I have a good security system at the newspaper office, and it extends to my apartment. I'll be fine."

"We have plenty of room here," Aurora said. "You can stay in Hawk's old room, or in Reed's. Or there is even a dedicated guest room, although I haven't cleaned it since Mama and Papa Coleman stayed there last weekend." She stroked her daughter's head. "I've been a little busy."

Bella couldn't help but smile; she hid it as quickly as she could. Watching Aurora with her daughter pulled at her heartstrings. If she stayed here there was every chance she would hold the baby, and that would not be good. She'd come to terms years ago that she would not be a mother. She was used to being alone, and that's what she wanted tonight.

"Thanks, but I'm going home." She stood and headed for the door. "Hawk, I'll see you in the morning."

She was almost to the stairs when Wyatt called out, "You need to take me to my truck."

"Walk!" She ran down the stairs as fast as she could, and as she headed out the door she thought about her purse. The fob needed to be near the ignition for her to be able to start her vehicle. Did anyone take her purse out of the car? If so she'd have to go back inside to get it, and she didn't want to do that.

Her purse was visible on the seat the minute she sat down. She started the car and headed toward the gate, where she faced her next obstacle—it was closed. She stopped about seven feet away. She knew she'd have to go back, which meant talking to Wyatt again. She slapped her palm against the steering wheel, and to her amazement the gate opened. She gunned the car and spun out onto the highway, praying no one was driving this way.

The road was empty, and it took her less than ten minutes to get to the newspaper office. She parked in the back near the stairs that led to her apartment. She turned off the car and stared out at the darkness. A death threat and having to deal with Wyatt on the same day. It jangled her nerves and made her wonder what in the hell she was doing back in Bookman Springs.

She should have stayed away, told her father no when he'd asked her to run the newspaper. It barely made enough money to cover a press run. Now that her father was dead she felt stuck here. Her mother constantly told her the people of Bookman Springs needed her, that the newspaper had to go on and her brothers couldn't do it. None of them knew the newspaper business like she did.

Plus, they had other jobs, other things to do. For a moment she wondered what it would take to convince her mother to sell the Gazette. If that happened, though, where would she go? There were many choices but every time she thought of one she came up with an excuse as to why it wouldn't work.

Did that mean that, deep down, she wanted to stay in Bookman Springs? Who knew the answer to that question? What she did know was she was lonely. Her friends from high school were all married and having babies, and spending time with them reminded her of what she didn't have.

There were too few eligible men in Bookman Springs, or ones she could see satisfying her needs There was only one in that area, and that was Wyatt Coleman... damn him. Wyatt had made her come harder than any man she'd ever dated, and he was a fantastic Dom, and a wonderful Daddy.

It was too bad he was an ass. If he wasn't, there was every chance they would be perfect together. Bella sighed in resignation and shook her head. They'd tried it once before, and it hadn't worked, because Wyatt wasn't able to keep it in his pants. Seeing him in the bar tonight proved he hadn't changed.

"Get out of the car and go upstairs," she said to the empty car. But before she could open the door something pounded on the hood.

"Holy shit!" she called out, only to hear laughter. "Damn you, Wyatt, get away from me!" There was no chance he had the time to get to the bar, retrieve his truck and make it here so fast.

"Not hardly," he said. He was standing by the car door now. "Until we figure out what's going on I'm your bodyguard. So get your ass out of the car and let's go upstairs. I hope you have food. I'm hungry."

Chapter 3

Wyatt bounded up the steel steps to the small landing. He pulled on the door handle, but it wouldn't turn in his hand.

"In the olden days you used to hide a key in a fake rock." He looked down. The motion light had come on when he'd come up the stairs, but its brightness revealed nothing. "Where is it hidden now?"

Below him, Bella stood near her car, with her hands on her hips. She glared up at him, and he couldn't help but smile. She was as spunky as ever, and it made his dick hard. But now was not the time for those thoughts. Hawk was sure someone was after them, that there was more to the missing relics than had been found. Wyatt would be damned if he would let anyone hurt the woman he still loved, the only woman he would ever love.

Their gazes locked, and he could feel the anger rolling off her. Finally he said, "I'm not going anywhere. Why don't you call the law and have them haul me off? I'll just be back. I can pick locks, you know."

"Like any good thief," she responded.

"No, just like any good juvenile delinquent. I learned how so I could break into the liquor cabinet at home." He shrugged. "I took my parents' liquor, so maybe I am a thief."

"How did you get here so fast?" she asked. "There is no way you could have made it to Rowdy's, retrieved your truck and made it here already."

"There are lots of trucks on the ranch," he said. "I'll get the one from the bar tomorrow."

He knew how stubborn she could be. She would probably stand down there all night, staring up at him. Of course he would stand here all night staring down at her.

"Whoever sent that note was angry," he said. "I'll behave myself." He held up two fingers, then added one, then another. He had no clue what hand signals like that meant. He'd never been a scout, or a member of any other organization. He smiled when she laughed.

"Like you know what that means," she said.

Bella started up the stairs, and he tried as hard as he could not to focus on her breasts, or her swaying hips. Tonight wasn't about sex. It was about keeping her safe.

Once she'd unlocked the door she stepped inside and he followed on her heels. Wyatt watched as she put a code into the keypad and he bit back a smile. The code was four numbers, 0422. His birthday. He wanted to point that out but he knew better. Before she turned to him he turned to survey the room. It was best she didn't notice he'd been watching.

"I can take care of myself," she said.

"What if the letter writer really meant yesterday?" he asked.

"Then we're doing him, or her, a favor by having both of us in the same place." She moved past him and dropped her purse in a chair. "Besides, why would they kill us before they have what they want? If there was something else taken from the museum that night then it is still missing. Whoever wrote that note thinks we have it. If they kill us they don't get what they want, because we won't be around to give it to them."

"Or they torture us for information." Wyatt plopped himself down on the sofa. "This place is nice. You've done a lot to it."

The apartment was like a loft, one big room that show-cased the living area, kitchen and dining room. There was a door against the far wall and he figured that was where the bedroom and bathroom were located.

"It gives me something to do…" Her words drifted off, and he wondered if she was about to add, "In this one-horse town." Sometimes he felt the same way, but it wasn't something he was willing to share.

"So, do you have food?" he asked.

"You're an uninvited guest." She sat down in a chair oppo-site the sofa. "You don't deserve food."

"Fine, I'll help myself." Within seconds he was in the kitchen. He opened the refrigerator to find it full. A quick survey showed various fruits and vegetables. There were jars of mayonnaise and mustard, plus containers of cold cuts, and a large package of bacon. There was also a plastic container, which he grabbed. There was only one thing this could be for his Bella. He pulled off the lid and smiled.

Cheese, lots of it.

"Quite a variety," he said.

"I'd thank you not to raid my refrigerator," she said. "In fact, I'd thank you to leave so I can go to bed."

"Past your bedtime?" He winked at her. "You know, if you're ready to go to bed I don't take up much room."

"You're a total bed hog," she said.

Wyatt snickered. "Used to be you didn't mind that about me."

"Used to be I thought you were a decent person."

Yeah, she had him there. He'd used and abused her, and

there was no excuse for it. Instead of responding he went to the cabinet. Once he opened it he found a box of crackers. A check of drawers found a cheese knife, which he took, along with the other items, into the living room.

"I like what you've done with the place," he said as he sat down. "Very—industrial. Concrete floors, saddles on sawhorses, walls full of reins and chaps. Are you considering opening a tack shop?"

"I won every piece of equipment in this apartment," she said. "But you know that. I'm going to ask you once more to leave. If you don't, I'm going to call the cops."

"Call my brother, then." Wyatt cut a slice of cheese and popped it in his mouth. "Oh, Gouda. Good choice."

Bella looked so frustrated that he considered going outside. He could sit in his truck and still watch the building, since the only way in was the front door. There were windows on the front part, but someone would have to either get on the roof and scale down to them, or put up a ladder to climb up. But her safety was more important than her frustration. If he sat in the truck he might fall asleep. It was better to stay inside the house where an opening door would wake him if he fell asleep.

"I'm not leaving," he said. "If you need to, call the sheriff and he can drag me out. You can print it on the front page of Wednesday's paper, above the fold if you want. And, of course, you can cover it on the web, too. It will drive up traffic on the site."

"I hate you," she said.

"Yeah, I think we've already established that." He ate another piece of cheese, then opened the box of crackers. The crinkle of the cellophane filled the silence that now stretched between them. He took out a few crackers, then looked at the cheese container. There was a block of what looked to be cheddar. He put the crackers on his thigh, then cut a piece from the block and made a cracker sandwich. Once he'd took a bite he said, "Sharp cheddar; another good choice."

"Are you going to review all my cheese choices, or are you going to leave?"

Wyatt got up and went back to the kitchen. He took a bottle of beer out of the fridge and twisted off the top. After he'd taken a healthy swig he said, "May I remind you that you came looking for me tonight. The letter obviously upset you enough that you didn't want to face this on your own. You came looking for me at the bar, on a Saturday night. You may hate me now, but you need me."

He'd been on the receiving end of that glare before, but this time there was a resignation to it that showed she believed what he said.

"Sorry I interrupted your blowjob."

"Only a hand job," he said. "That girl has never sucked my dick."

"Are you telling me you've been celibate since we broke up?"

"Have you?" he asked. She didn't answer and he crossed back into the living area and sat down. "I'm a ho-dog, remember? She might have been jerking me off, but her mouth had been nowhere near my cock." He wanted to tell her there had never been another woman in his life who affected him the way she did. Even when he was with another woman he usually thought of her, which was unfair to the women, he knew. He'd tried twice to forge a relationship with a woman who would make a good sub, and little, for him, but he'd been unsuccessful both times.

There had never been another woman he loved. But she wouldn't believe him. Sometimes he found it hard to believe himself.

To try and change the direction his thoughts were taking he fixed himself another cheese/cracker sandwich. As he crunched he said, "I'm not leaving, unless one of the sheriff's deputies drags me out of here in handcuffs."

After another swig of his beer he looked up at her. She stood near one of the saddles she'd won in her barrel racing days. As much as he tried to keep on the straight and narrow he thought of bending her over the saddle, whipping her ass and then fucking her until she fainted. His cock stirred under his jeans, and he turned his attention back to the food.

It was either that or tackle her and fuck them both senseless.

"Fine," she finally said. "But I want you out of here before anyone sees your truck in front of my house."

He snorted in laughter. "Darlin', half the customers at Rowdy's saw me hog-tie you and throw you in the back of your SUV. By tomorrow morning the whole town will think we're up here fucking. Maybe that will deter the letter writer."

Without answering, Bella stalked toward her bedroom.

"Can I have a pillow and blanket?" he asked.

"Go get them from the ranch," she called out, right before she slammed her bedroom door.

When she was gone, Wyatt continued to eat and drink. His mind whirled around memories of them losing their virginity to each other so long ago, and the incredible years that followed. Of course there was also the disastrous break-up, and the memory of how he'd hurt her.

Maybe, just maybe, he could make it up to her now. Maybe she would take him back.

In your dreams, he thought. But sometimes dreams became reality. More than likely, though, this one would be a nightmare, and she would toss him out on his ass once they got to the bottom of the threat.

"Shit, shit, shit."

"Do you mind, I have young children around me."

Bella stared at her phone. "Are you shitting me? Did you hear what I said? I'm in crisis mode here. Wyatt is in the living area, and I feel as if I'm hyperventilating."

"Find a paper bag."

Bella shook the phone and said, "Rosa, are you listening to me? You're my best friend and you're cracking jokes. I called you for support, not fucking sarcasm."

"I told you, quit cussing around my children." Rosa snorted in laughter.

"Have you got me on speaker? And it's also midnight. What are your kids doing up so late?"

Bella knew it was late, much too late to call her bestie, who was now married with three kids. But she had to talk to someone about the hunk of man sitting just behind the closed door.

"Julia has colic, and her crying woke up Russell and Ray."

"And me!" Rosa's husband, Frank, yelled in the background.

"Sorry, I'll let you go."

Bella took the phone away from her ear and was about to hit end call when she heard Rosa call out, "Don't hang up!"

She brought the phone back to her ear. "I'm sorry it's so late. I just… I just…" She needed a shot of tequila is what she needed, but that was in the other room. She'd already had to go in there to get her purse and phone. There was no way she was going back.

"Take a deep breath, Bella," Rosa said. "Then tell me exactly what happened, and don't leave out any details."

"What about the babies?" Bella asked.

"Frank can handle it. Now, spill."

Bella sat down in the middle of the bed. She pushed thoughts of sharing this space with Wyatt out of her mind, then said, "Well, you know how my Dad hid the stolen arti-facts? I've told you about that, right?"

When Rosa said yes, Bella told her everything, about the letter, about going in search of Wyatt, and about him following her home and camping out on the couch.

"I want to kick him out, but he won't leave," Bella said.

There was a silence, and Bella knew Rosa was marshaling her thoughts. Finally she said, "We need to break this conver-sation into two parts, one about the threat, and the other about Wyatt."

"Let's talk about the letter, so I can hang up on you while you talk about Wyatt."

Rosa chuckled. "Here's my thing. You have to figure out who wrote the letter…"

Before she could continue Bella said, "Because whoever wrote the letter stole the artifacts."

"Exactly," Rosa said. "You just have to figure out who it was; and the way you do that is by putting your skills as an investigative journalist to the test."

Bella truly laughed for the first time that night. "Rosa, I run a weekly newspaper that prints gossip columns about who has out of town visitors and who won the pie contest at the community center that week."

Trying to figure out who had stolen the artifacts had not been high on her list. There was a part of her that wondered if her father had a hand in the theft. She didn't want to think that, but he had hidden them, which meant he knew who did it. Could she use investigative journalism skills to figure out whodunit, and therefore was angry the items had been given to the tribe and they'd lost out on any profit they might get from selling them?

"What's the deal with 'you have it, give it to me'," Rosa said.

"No clue," Bella answered. "That's something else to get to the bottom of."

"How would you do that, exactly?" Rosa asked.

Bella couldn't help but laugh. "Obviously using my investigative skills." She hated to admit the idea of figuring things out was intriguing. Or it would be if she didn't have the death threat hanging over her head.

"You're going to have to put on your big girl panties and get to the bottom of things," Rosa said. Before Bella could answer, she said, "And now there's the other thing. Bella, you've been my best friend for almost thirty years now. So you can trust me to speak the truth to you."

"I don't like where this is going," Bella said. "I called you for support, not a lecture."

"Well you're going to get both." Rosa sighed and said, "One second."

Bella could hear her talking again, but the sounds were muffled. She imagined Rosa sitting in the kitchen on the ranch she shared with her husband, talking to him about the kids. Bella could no longer hear the children in the background.

"Okay, they're asleep," Rosa said. "Now, the first thing I want to say is you need to be careful. Someone who writes a death threat is crazy. There is no telling what they will do. So if you turn down Wyatt's offer of protection, I'm going to come to Bookman Springs and slap the shit out of you."

Bella smiled. "What's the second thing?"

"Sweetie, you know I love you, but there is a reason you went looking for Wyatt."

"Yeah, to warn him," Bella said.

"On a Saturday night?"

Bella could almost see Rosa shaking her head. "You may not want to forgive him for being an ass to you, but you need to. You love him. You need him in your life."

"I hate him," Bella said.

"Actions speak louder than words," Rosa said. "The first thing you did when you got that letter was run to warn him."

"Now I hate you," Bella said.

"For pointing out the obvious," Rosa said. "Let him fuck you. How long has it been for you? A year? Longer? Plus he likes that weird stuff you like. Let him tie you up and do all that crazy shit. You know you want it."

"Now I really hate you," Bella said.

"Don't hate me for telling you the truth," Rosa said. "Think about why you went to Rowdy's in the first place, and you'll know I'm telling you the truth. If you continue to lie to yourself, you'll just be miserable."

"Yeah, thanks for that." Bella ran her free hand through her dark hair. "Go sleep with your husband."

Rosa chuckled. "Go sleep with the man you love."

The phone went dead, and Bella tossed it on the bed beside her. She had loved Wyatt at one point, loved him so fiercely she thought she'd die without him. And then IT had happened… and he'd proved he really didn't care for her; that the only thing he wanted from her was sex.

No, she wouldn't go through that again. Because this time she didn't think she'd make it through.

Chapter 4

Coffee. The smell hit her square in the face and made her sit up and sniff. One glance at the window showed the sun wasn't even up yet. She'd barely slept last night because all she could do was think about Rosa's advice.

Go jump his bones. It will release some of that tension you're feeling. He likes that freaky stuff that you like.

It had taken every inch of willpower she had to stay in her bedroom because every time she closed her eyes she saw Wyatt standing in front of her, belt in hand, demanding she bend over the bed. At one point she could swear she felt the sting of the leather hitting her ass. When that had happened she'd gotten up, gone to her closet where she hid her Little things, and turned on the light. She sat at the table and colored until she'd finally fallen asleep. She'd barely woken and crawled into bed when the smell of the coffee hit her.

She glanced at the alarm clock that sat across the room. It was just after five. What the hell was he doing up so early? Then it hit her. Wyatt worked the ranch. He was probably up this early every day of the week.

Bella rolled over and pulled the pillow over her head. There was a reason she kept her alarm clock on the other side of the room—if there was one thing she wasn't it was a morning person. She never made it to the office until around ten. As much as she loved country life, and riding horses, she could not handle the ranch life—up at dawn every day.

She groaned, and then sniffed the air. Was that bacon she smelled? Other than cheese and eggs, that was the only food in her refrigerator. So he was going to deplete her cheese stash, and eat all her bacon and eggs? There was bread in the cupboard, but that was about all. She never cooked. Being by herself it was easier to eat out, or make a sandwich, paired with macaroni and cheese.

Bella ate a lot of sandwiches.

"What the hell?" Wyatt's voice rang out and Bella sighed. She would never get back to sleep now.

She got up, threw on her robe and went into the main room. Wyatt stood at the stove, bare chested. She prayed he had on jeans.

Before she could say anything he said, "You only have two slices of bread."

She watched as he dropped the two slices in the toaster. "Those are for me," she said. "Go home and eat biscuits and gravy. If I remember right, Austin cooks that on Sunday mornings."

The thought made her mouth water. She loved Austin's cooking.

"We'll have the biscuits once we arrive at the ranch," he said. She watched as he flipped the bacon. Arguing with him would get her nowhere. He would only hogtie her, and kidnap her once again.

"We can't spend 24/7 together, you know," she said. "I have a job. You have a job."

He flipped the bacon once more. When the toast popped

up he pulled the slices from their slot. "Yeah, I've thought about that. I think you'll be safe at the newspaper, as long as you don't go running around during the day. You can stay there until I can leave the ranch. If you want we can stay here, but I prefer staying at the ranch. The security is better there."

"Yeah, it's like Fort Knox." She couldn't wait anymore. If she was going to be up this early she needed coffee. She went to the cabinet, took down a cup, pulled her flavored creamer from the refrigerator and put a substantial portion of it in her cup before adding the coffee.

"You haven't changed," Wyatt said with a laugh.

"I noticed you're putting up a taller fence," she said. "Why?"

"We had a break-in recently," he said.

"Really? It wasn't on the reports from the sheriff's department, and Hawk didn't mention it to me when I asked him what had been going on lately."

"It was no big deal," Wyatt said. He put the bacon strips on a paper towel, then cracked eggs into the grease.

"Big enough to make you put in a new fence," she said. "What gives?"

"Nothing." The edge in his tone told her there was something there. She would have to work to get it out of him. She'd always thought something was going on out there. During her years with Wyatt, there had been secret talks, and conversations that stopped the minute she stepped into the room. She'd always thought they'd been talking about her, but now she wondered what was really taking place behind those fences—besides rescuing horses.

He scrambled the eggs, adding salt and pepper. "Do you have some salsa in the fridge?"

"Open the door and see," she said.

"If the eggs burn, you get the really charred parts." He

put down his fork and went to the refrigerator, returning moments later with a jar of salsa.

Bella watched as he plated two servings, putting one slice of bread on each. Then he sat at the table, which was piled with papers and books on one side, and started to eat.

"Join me," he said. "Then we can shower together and scrub each other's backs."

"It's too early to eat," she said. "You can have my share, and I'll go shower."

She hurried to the bedroom and locked the door, then went to the bathroom, which had a doorway to the bedroom and one to the main part of the apartment, and locked the outside door so Wyatt couldn't get in. Seeing him in such a calm, domestic situation, cooking breakfast and then eating it, brought back more memories that pulled at her heart. She once again thought of Rosa's words last night, *let him protect you, and fuck you. You need it and he likes that freaky shit that you like.*

She never should have gone to look for Wyatt last night. She should have called Hawk and reported it to law enforcement. That would have kept her from being in such close proximity with Wyatt, because she knew him well enough to know he wouldn't drop things until they got to the bottom of the letter.

Bella wasn't sure she could resist him that long. It would take every ounce of will power she had, and right now, that wasn't very much.

Wyatt dropped half a bale of hay in the center of the pen before he crossed to the gate that connected the pen to the stables. This area was where they kept the horses that had been on the ranch for a while, ones that were starting to heal. Each horse that came to the Rescue Ranch came from a different situation.

He opened the gate and whistled. Four of the six occupants came out of their stalls and ambled to the mound of hay. He watched as they started to eat.

Although he and Austin worked the horses, Kyle was the true horse whisperer. If they had a problem dealing with a horse, if it needed more care than its stable mates, they would call in their brother. Kyle had always been able to calm down horses that were having a less than good day. His connection with animals was one of the reasons he'd become a vet, Wyatt thought.

Austin was good with animals too, but better in the kitchen. Right now he was entertaining Bella, which was what Wyatt would rather be doing. But Austin had planned a Sunday lunch, and he needed to be working on it, which was why Wyatt was out here on his own. He didn't like the idea that Bella was in the house, chatting up his brothers. He'd asked her to come out with him, but she'd refused, her excuse being that she hadn't had enough coffee to operate as a human being yet.

It wasn't that he thought she would try to hit on Austin to make him jealous. It was that he didn't trust her not to ask probing questions about the fence and why they were raising the height to seven feet. The reason he'd given her about a thief was true. Several weeks ago, someone had climbed the fence and made their way into the house so they could steal a purse, belonging to his brother Reed's then girlfriend, now wife.

The theft had shown a glaring error in the ranch's security. They did more than rescue horses here—they also operated a state-funded operation where ladies who were in abusive relationships had a place to hide while they figured out the next moves in their lives.

He hadn't told Bella about that aspect of the ranch when they were first lovers because his parents had been running it, and it hadn't been that large of an operation. Plus, his father had threatened them with hours of mucking out stalls if they told anyone. Their mother, who had lost a sister to domestic violence, had been nicer about the whole thing, telling them how important it was to keep the secret so the ladies were not found.

Now they had six cabins, with the plan to add four more in the next year. As a matter of fact, Holt was meeting with a contractor tomorrow morning to price the additions. They had a den mother who watched over the ladies and their families and no one in town knew about it except for Mags, who ran the local supermarket. She herself had been a client back in his parents' day, and she was not about to let the secret out.

He thought Bella would keep the secret if she knew, too, but it wasn't a decision he could make on his own. The six brothers ran the ranch, with Holt being the head of things. Before Wyatt told Bella, he would have to clear it with his brothers. Since she was the editor/publisher of the paper, he was pretty sure they would say no. Not because they didn't trust her, but because they wanted as few people as possible to know.

Hopefully, she wasn't inside asking Austin leading questions that would make him think Wyatt had already told her about the confidential part of the ranch. It wasn't that he didn't trust his brother. He just knew Bella could worm information out of anyone. She was crafty that way.

There were two more horses to feed. Both of them were new and being kept in isolation for their own safety. One was so abused she'd kicked out slats from her stall twice already and she'd only been here a few days. She never came to eat when he put the hay in her corral. Instead she stared at him, her gaze jaded.

Wyatt mounted his horse and rode to the isolation stalls. The first one was easy. The beautiful roan here had been starved, and when he put down hay, the horse came running. Austin had placed several bales down here so they didn't have to haul every day. He threw hay into the stall and watched as the gorgeous black and white pinto stuck her muzzle out and sniffed the air.

"Come and eat, and I have a treat for you afterward," Wyatt said. He had several apples in his saddlebags. He straddled the fence and sat on the top board, one leg on either side. The horse, which he'd named Sadie, continued to stare at him. "Come on, girl, I'm not going to hurt you."

"Too bad you can't promise me the same thing."

He turned to see Bella sitting atop Austin's big, white Arabian. The horse stood seventeen hands high, which was large for its breed, and she looked tiny in comparison. His cock stirred as their gazes locked. The thought of pulling her off the horse, throwing her to her hands and knees and fucking her until she fainted took over.

"You never complained when I hurt you before," he said. "Well, physically hurt you that is."

The tension in the air was thick. She nudged the horse closer to where he sat, and out of the corner of his eye, Wyatt saw Sadie come out of her stall. The horse sniffed the air, and then her gaze focused on the hay. She was obviously hungry, and he was keeping her from eating. But if he moved, would she retreat back into her pen.

He put his finger to his lips as he looked back at Bella. She nodded and stayed in place. Sadie started to eat; every few bites she glanced at Wyatt, and then at Bella.

"Is this a first?" Bella asked, softly.

"It is," Wyatt said. "I did tell her I had treats for her if she ate." He inclined his head toward his horse. "I have apples for her in my saddlebag… granny smiths. Your favorite."

Her smile was her only response, and it warmed Wyatt's heart. She pulled gently on Lawrence's reins and sidestepped her way over to where his horse stood grazing on the grass. Once there she reached into his saddlebag and pulled out two apples. She tossed one in his direction and he caught it, and the second one that followed. When she had a third one in her hand, she slowly walked Lawrence to where Wyatt sat. He had already taken out his knife and started to cut the first apple. Once he'd quartered it and taken out the seeds, he fed a quarter to Lawrence. Blaze had obviously smelled the treat because he was now next to Lawrence; he whinnied softly and Wyatt gave him a quarter.

"Look," Bella whispered. Sadie had come up, standing about four feet from where the group of horses and people had gathered. "You've done well with her."

"I can't claim the credit," Wyatt said. "Kyle has been down here working with her."

"What happened to her?" Bella asked.

"Kyle says she has scars, as if she was beaten." Wyatt held out a quarter of the apple, but Sadie ignored it. "She was abandoned in a field near Wichita Falls. One of the sheriff's deputies there is friends with Hawk, and he called us."

He wiggled the apple at Sadie, but she continued to ignore it.

"Can't charm her, huh?" The humor in Bella's voice was a challenge.

"Perhaps I can charm you." He cocked his head. "Speaking of charming, how did you get Austin to let you ride Lawrence? He never lets anyone ride his horse."

"I smiled at him," she said.

Wyatt narrowed his eyes at her. "You're being very nice for someone who doesn't really want to be here."

"Why fight the inevitable?" She fixed him with a sweet smile, one he hadn't seen in a long time. "I'm going for a ride now."

Before he could offer to join her she took off, pushing Lawrence to a run, which made Sadie run back to her stall. Since she was heading back toward the house he didn't go after her. He did need to talk to Holt about telling Bella about the cabins before she found them on her own.

Wyatt got down from the fence. He tossed the apples onto the remaining hay. There were a few more in the saddle bags, and he planned on cutting one up for Blaze.

"Come eat your treat," he said to Sadie. She stared at him but didn't budge. "I'll just leave it there." He climbed to the other side of the fence. As he neared his horse, the shake of his mane let Wyatt know Blaze wasn't happy with his small quarter. "Just a minute fella." He patted him on the neck and Blaze shook his head, his mane flying.

"Hold on, hold on," he said. He stopped and stepped up to look Blaze in the face. "She was very subdued, wasn't she? That's not like Bella."

Blaze shook his head again as if to say, "No shit, Sherlock."

Wyatt went to Blaze's side and reached into his saddlebag and found three more apples. He took one out, but something told him things were not right. The bags were useful to carry water, his keys and his phone. He put his hand back inside.

"Son of a fucking bitch," he said. He moved his hands around but found no keys, or phone. He quickly crossed to the other side, but found only a few bottles of water in the bag.

The little minx had stolen his phone, and his keys, while she was getting the apples. He hadn't picked up his truck from Rowdy's parking lot, but there were several ranch trucks she could take to get off the property—and he didn't have his phone to warn the guys to watch her. He quickly mounted Blaze and took off after her.

She had a head start, but he was pretty sure he knew where she was going. Hopefully he would find her quickly, and spank her ass for stealing from him.

Chapter 5

"Where is it? Where is it?" Bella sat in her stolen—no, borrowed—truck, wondering how to get the gate open. There was no box to put in a code, which to her meant there was a clicker somewhere. She checked the visor, the glove compartment and the console between the seats. There was nothing.

Maybe all the brothers had a button on their key fob. She knew time was ticking away. By now Wyatt had figured out she'd stolen his keys and phone and he would be hot on her trail.

"Breath deep, calm down," she said. "Think about how he opened the gate when you arrived this morning." She closed her eyes and thought about the drive. She'd been quiet because she was angry that she'd not been given a choice in the trip. She'd wanted to stay home and do research on the museum theft. She could have used the ranch's Wi-Fi to do what she needed; in fact, Austin had given her the password. But she wanted to be at home, where she was comfortable.

She hadn't gone riding with the intention of stealing Wyatt's keys, but when she'd seen them in the saddlebag instinct had taken over. She'd taken his phone so he couldn't call and warn Austin to keep her from leaving.

"Think, think!" She remembered the trip over, of Wyatt lowering his left hand between the seat and the door. She did the same and her hand dropped into the door compartment, where she found the clicker. Bella pointed it at the gate and clicked, and the gate started to swing open. She willed it to hurry, and when she was on the other side she pressed the clicker one more time, and the gate started to close.

The highway stretched out in front of her, and the consequences of what she'd just done hit her square in the face. She hadn't gone back in the house to retrieve her purse, so she didn't have her phone, or the keys to her car or house. She had no plan, but as she took off down the highway, one came to mind. She would drive to Frank's house. She and her brother were close, and he would help her find a place where she could hide from Wyatt.

Hiding. It wasn't something she wanted to do, but she needed a place to think, a place to do her research. She could hide out there for a while, drink coffee and be Aunt Bella to Frank's two young children. That wouldn't get her research done, but it would make her smile.

As she drove through town she prayed she didn't run into Hawk, who would wonder why she was driving a ranch truck. As she hit the city limits she breathed a sigh of relief as she headed east toward Frank's spread. Things were going well. Until the phone rang. She debated about whether to answer it. She picked it up from the passenger seat and looked at the display—it read Austin.

Answer, decline. The buttons seemed to flash before her eyes. Instead of pressing one she dropped the phone back on the seat.

"Don't talk and drive," she said to the empty cab.

Frank's spread was about ten miles out of town. She

turned onto the farm-to-market road that would lead to the gate, which stood open, unlike the gate at the Rescue Ranch. She once again wondered about that fact, mixed with the fence that was being elevated. What exactly were they guarding in there? Fragments of UFOs? Were they operating a brothel? Or did Wyatt actually have whatever the letter writer was seeking and didn't want to give it back?

Once she was at the house she put the vehicle in park and picked up the phone. The display showed only one missed call and no message.

"What are you doing driving a Rescue Ranch truck?" Frank called out from the porch. He had a coffee mug in his hand.

"My car is… out of commission for a while," she said as she got out.

"And you borrowed a truck from the ranch?" He took a drink from his cup. "From Wyatt? Are the two of you back together?"

"Never."

"Then what are you doing with a Rescue Ranch truck?"

Before she could answer the door behind Frank flew open. "Aunt Bella!" Three-year-old Bonnie flew out the door and ran down the stairs.

"Hey Bonnie!" Bella gathered her niece in her arms and twirled her around.

"What did you bring me?" Bonnie asked.

"See, that's what happens when you bring her something every time you come out," Frank said. "Bonnie, don't ask for things. It's rude."

Bella wanted to tell Frank not to tell Bonnie that, because it made Bella think she was getting her niece in trouble. There was a consequence to being spoiled. Her father and brothers generally gave her everything she wanted, and because of that she expected everything to be perfect; she expected to get anything she wanted, and life didn't always happen that way. Hopefully it wasn't too late for her to teach Bonnie that lesson.

"Right now my gift will be my time," Bella said. "How about we play jacks?"

"Yes, yes," Bonnie said. She grabbed Bella's hand and tried to pull her toward the house.

"Just a minute, BB," Frank said. "I need to talk to your Aunt Bella for minute. Do me a favor and go check on Mama and JB."

"Okay." Bonnie dropped Bella's hand and ran for the door.

"You really should teach your children their names," Bella said. "When they get to school their teachers won't call them by their initials."

"Tell me why you're in a Rescue Ranch truck," Frank said.

"I told you, my car is out of commission." Bella shrugged. "Can I use your office to do some work?"

"Did you steal that truck?" Frank glared at her, and Bella fought the urge to get back in the vehicle and leave.

"I have the keys," Bella said with a laugh. "It's borrowed, that's all. Can I use your office, or not?"

"What's wrong with yours?"

Before she could answer, Frank's phone rang. He pulled it from his pocket and chuckled. "That app that identifies all numbers is worth the money." He pressed the screen and Wyatt's voice filled the air.

"Don't let her leave," Wyatt said. "If she does, remind her of the death threat against the two of us."

The phone went dead and Frank glared at her. "Death threat?"

"How did he find me so fast?" Bella didn't wait for Frank to answer what was really just her musing out loud. She ran toward the driver's side door of the truck, but before she could open it, a truck pulled up behind her 'borrowed' vehicle. The driver's side door of the new vehicle opened, and the flash of a star let her know the vehicle belonged to Hawk Coleman, the county constable.

"Fuck," she muttered.

"Are you going to jail?" Frank asked.

"That depends," Hawk said. Seconds later another truck pulled up and Wyatt practically jumped out of the vehicle.

Bella pointed at Wyatt. "He kidnapped me, twice!"

"Twice?" Hawk asked with a laugh. "Last I heard it was only once. You're an overachiever little brother. Or you're just really bad at it."

"You're a car thief!" Wyatt pointed at her.

"Which is worse, taking a car or keeping a person against their will?" Bella pointed at him.

"He's obviously not good at keeping you if he had to do it twice," Hawk said.

"That'll change," Wyatt countered. "Tonight I'll tie her to the bed."

"I don't want to hear about your sex life," Hawk said. He laughed, and Bella wanted to say it wasn't a joke.

"Enough!" Frank called out. "Does someone want to tell me what the hell is going on here? Death threats? Kidnappings? Stolen trucks? Somebody needs to tell me what's going on right damn now."

Bella glared at Wyatt. What had she been thinking when she'd gone to Rowdy's last night? And when she'd gone with him this morning? And when she'd come out here? She should have gone somewhere they wouldn't have found her so fast.

"How'd you find me?" she asked.

"GPS," Hawk said, "in both the truck and the phone."

"Somebody tell me what the hell's going on!" Frank yelled.

"Let's go inside," Hawk said. "There's a lot to tell."

Frank went inside, and Hawk followed him. When they were gone, Wyatt stepped up next to her.

"You've earned yourself a damn hard spanking," Wyatt said.

"Fuck you," she spat out at him.

"Not tonight," he said. "Tonight will be about punishment. You can't steal a truck and think I'm just going to look the other way."

"I borrowed it," she said with a laugh. "And I'll be staying with my brother, not with you tonight."

Wyatt's chuckle made her spine tingle. "We'll see about that," he said. "We'll see."

The whole thing was getting way out of hand. She hadn't expected it to blow up the way it had. If life was how it should be she would be at home right now eating cheese and maybe watching some TV.

But here she was at the Rescue Ranch once again with not only all the Colemans around her but her family as well, all three of her brothers and her mother, who looked as if she might blow up at any moment.

They were all at the Rescue Ranch, about to feast on the recipe Austin was trying, some sort of stacked enchiladas that he'd never made before. Frank and Hawk had set up the meeting. She remembered the look on her brother's face when she'd finally come into the house after Wyatt and Hawk had arrived. It was a mixture of anger and concern, and she hadn't been able to tell which one was at the forefront. Before she knew it her brothers Sam and Jesse were there, and everyone was making decisions about what needed to happen next—everyone but her. Every time she tried to butt into the conversation she'd been ignored.

Only Wyatt had paid attention to her. In fact he'd stared at her constantly, and it was easy to read his expression. He was pissed; so angry she was surprised he didn't sit down and take her over his knee right then and there.

He'd behaved, though, and he was doing so right now. He had a plate full of tortilla chips and a cup of salsa, and every once in a while he stared at her. She could still read his expression; he was not happy with her.

There was a time when she welcomed that look, one she'd come to think of as his Daddy look. It meant she'd done something bad and would face the consequences. If there was a time when she would be alone with him tonight she was sure that would be the case. But she had already made sure that wouldn't happen. She'd talked to Frank that afternoon and asked if she could stay at his house. He'd told her yes, so that's where she would be tonight, so that meant no spanking.

Although she might physically want a spanking, and the feelings it brought about, she didn't want to deal with the mental pain it would bring. She was over losing Wyatt, no matter what Rosa said. She didn't want to open herself up to him again, because losing him the first time had almost killed her. If she had to go through it again she was sure she would not survive.

"You're awfully quiet for the person who has caused all this commotion."

Bella took a drink of her tea, and wished that when Austin had offered she'd taken that beer. "Oh Mother, I'm just a big old troublemaker. I'm just waiting to watch people scream at each other so I can sit back and laugh."

"Don't you take that tone with me young lady."

"I'm sorry, Mother, I don't know any other tone when I'm being accused of starting a problem, which is exactly what you are doing."

"Did you?" Before Bella could answer her mother continued, "It's bad enough people know your father hid those stolen items, but for you to make up this garbage to try and get back with your former lover? How could you embarrass your family this way?"

It was as if she'd been kicked in the stomach. "You think I'm making this up?"

"Why didn't you just ask him to take you back?" her mother asked. "I'm sure he would have considered it."

And there was another kick, this one in the teeth. "Thanks for your faith in me, Mother. I assure you I have not made this up."

"Lower your voice," Bitsy said. "People are staring."

Bella looked around the room. Sure enough, people were staring, but she didn't care. "Fuck them! You just accused me of making this up so I could get laid."

"Bella Louise!" Frank's voice rang out. "Show some respect."

"Why? She's not showing any to me." Bella poked herself in the chest. "I was taught respect is a two-way street. What am I supposed to do, cow down to being accused of trying to wiggle back into Wyatt's life? I assure you this is real, and the fact my own mother doesn't believe in me really hurts."

"This is not the place," Frank said.

Before he could continue, Bella said, "Why not? She accused me here. Everyone is here to decide what is best for me. Am I supposed to just take it all in and keep my mouth shut? Well, screw you all. I'm out of here."

She bolted out the door. Several people, including her mother and Frank, called out for her to stop. But she kept going. When she got to the bottom of the stairs she realized that, once again, she hadn't really thought this through. She didn't have her purse, which included her keys. Of course her car was at her house, and something told her she wouldn't be able to 'borrow' a Rescue Ranch truck again.

"Hey." The sound of Wyatt's voice sent dread through her.

He would jump her, too, she knew. After all, he was still angry with her about the truck.

But when she turned to him she was surprised to find him standing there with her purse in his hands. "Let's get out of here. But first let's go to the kitchen and steal food that Austin might have left there. I'm hungry."

Chapter 6

An hour later, Bella sat on her couch, a cheeseboard on the coffee table. Wyatt had driven through the only fast-food place in town and bought himself a few hamburgers. Then he'd gone to the convenience store and bought some beer. Now, as she stared at her favorite snack, her stomach did not respond, at least not in the feed me way.

"Want a cheeseburger?" Wyatt asked between bites. "Or some of these fatty, salty fries?"

What was he doing in her house again? He'd rescued her from a bad situation, true, but she'd intended to find a way to slip away from him. She didn't want to be sitting here eating with him.

"We should have bought milkshakes." She stared at the cheese. "It's not too late. You could go and get a get me one— vanilla, please."

"I can see the wheels inside your brain moving," he said. "If you think I'm going out that door so you can lock it behind me, you're nuts."

Bella watched as he scarfed down another burger.

"I'm going to make one for myself," she said. She got up

and went into the kitchen. After she pulled out the blender she took ice cream from the freezer.

"Be careful of the sweets," Wyatt said. "You're going to be over my knee before long. Being spanked with a belly full of ice cream might not be a good idea."

"According to you," Bella said, "I haven't done anything wrong."

"Punishment for stealing the truck, if you remember," Wyatt countered.

"Borrowing," Bella said. "That's what happens when you force someone to stay some place they don't want to be."

"Don't blame your illegal actions on someone trying to keep you safe."

"You mean someone trying to restrict my movement." She scooped several large dollops of ice cream into the blender. She added some milk and a little splash of vanilla extract.

"Your spanking is not my fault," he said.

Bella turned on the blender to try and drown out his words. She was tempted to pour the shake over his head, but that would be a waste of good ice cream. But she still had milk in the carton. If he threatened her once more she might just let him have a glass, or two. The more he droned on about her behaving herself, and how she'd obviously forgotten the manners he'd taught her when they were together before, the more drowning him in milk made her smile. It would be a mess to clean up, but it would be worth it. But cleaning up milk would not be fun, and if she missed some it would start to stink after a while, depending on how much she missed. Bella retrieved a straw and a spoon from the drawer and tasted her creamy concoction. It was silky on her tongue and slid gently down her throat.

The treat provided a calming effect she desperately needed, since she still wanted nothing more than to drown Wyatt in something wet.

"Hey babe, can you get me another beer?" He held the longneck up between his thumb and index finger and wiggled it back and forth.

"Babe?" she said.

"Bella?" he said. "Does that sound better?"

"I'm not your maid, you know," she said. "Get it yourself."

"Somebody's got her knickers in a twist," he said.

"I think I've made it quite clear," she began. "I don't want you in my life. I can take care of myself. I warned you about the death threat, and that was my intent. For my thanks I've fought with my brother and my mother, and you're sitting on my couch acting as if you own the place."

"All I'm asking for is a beer to wash down my burgers." He jiggled the bottle again. "And you know I'm not leaving, so you might as well get used to it. I'm not leaving this chair, except to move to the couch to sleep, after I spank your ass for stealing the truck."

"Not leaving the chair, huh?" she said under her breath. "Stay where you are then, and I'll be a gracious hostess." She took a longneck out of the refrigerator and shook it. She walked up behind him and pointed it at the back of his neck, twisted off the top and let the spray soak him.

"Son of a bitch." He jumped up from the seat, the uneaten fries and a half-eaten burger slipping from the paper plate on his lap and dropping to the floor. Bella put her thumb over the opening and shook the bottle again. This time she aimed the spray higher and got him straight in the face.

"Since you didn't plan on leaving that chair, I thought I'd give you a shower," she said. "Just trying to be helpful. And you're not spanking me. Those days are over."

"The fuck they are," Wyatt said. He flung himself down on the couch, grabbing her around the waist as he fell. Bella was never sure how he did it so expertly, but as he'd done when they were together she was across his lap quickly and efficiently. He slapped her ass and even through her jeans the swat stung like the dickens.

He smacked her ass once more, and she cried out in frustration. "Stop it! You fucking asshole!"

"Such a mouth," he said as he continued to swat her. "You have this coming and you know it. Or perhaps you would like it better if I let Hawk arrest you for stealing the truck. Would you let one of your underlings write the story, or would you do it? I can see the headline now, above the fold, of course, 'Publisher arrested for grand theft auto'. Do you think some young pup will design a video game out of it?"

He spanked her harder, the sound of his hand slamming down on her ass filling the room. It didn't seem as if he were letting up, but she remembered that about him. He could go on forever, his hand taking it much longer than her bottom could withstand it. And it was even worse when he was using a belt, or another implement.

Bella tried to wiggle out of his grasp, but he held her close and continued his 'penalty'.

"I hate you! I hate you!"

"I'm not looking for love by doing this," Wyatt said. "This is about discipline and punishment. I thought I'd taught you better when we were together."

Bella managed to twist enough to look up at him. One of his slaps landed on the side of her thigh and it stung something fierce.

"Watch it!"

"Blame yourself," Wyatt said. "You're the one who moved."

"Only so I could respond to the 'teach me' reference. What you taught me was you were always more attracted to other women than to me. We can ask Paisley, or what was the name of the other woman you were screwing when I found the three of you? I can't remember because she wasn't from around here. But you found a home in her pussy, didn't you? Or was it her ass? Or her mouth? Or all three? Or can't you remember back that far?"

The look of utter shock on his face made her smile. It gave her the upper hand and that was what she wanted. She would not allow herself to go down the Wyatt Coleman road again.

"Get up," he said tersely.

"What's wrong? Don't you like to be reminded that you can be a total shit?"

"You don't think I know that already? I apologized when it happened." He shook his head ever so slightly. "I can apologize again, but it won't do a world of good."

"It'll do me good to hear it," she countered.

"Then I'm sorry," Wyatt said. "More sorry than you'll ever know."

"I think what you want to say is sorrier than I'll ever know."

"Thank you, madam editor, for correcting my English," he said.

"Glad to be of service," she said, slyly. "Now, stop slapping my ass because you don't have that right anymore. If you want to punish me for the truck thing figure out something else."

"I will," he said. "You can get up now."

"Gee, thanks for your permission." She slid off his lap and landed on her knees next to him. She hated to admit that from this position her mouth was near his cock. She had great memories of sucking him, of taking him deep into her mouth and feeling him swell and then shoot off.

Wyatt stroked her hair, which made the physical desire she felt swell.

"See something you like down there?" he asked.

"Don't flatter yourself," she replied. "Every man I know wears jeans, and that's what I'm seeing."

"Are you asking me to take my dick out?" Wyatt put his hands on the button of his jeans. "I can do that."

"Don't bother." Bella stood and put her hands on her hips. "If you feel the need, go out to the bar and find your little chippy from Saturday night. I'm sure she'd love to see your dick. I haven't missed it."

Liar, she said to herself. You're a huge liar. And the worst part is he knows you well enough to know you're lying.

"Take it out!" she wanted to scream. It had been so long since she'd had sex that even looking at his cock would be incredible. But looking at it would make her want to take him inside her, and she would be damned if she would give him that satisfaction. It was time to change the subject.

"We need to talk about tomorrow," she said. "I understand you want to protect me, but I have a job, and so do you. You can't follow me around all day."

"You can come to the ranch."

Before she could answer he held up his hand. "I know that's not going to work, but right now a great deal of the blood flow to my brain is being diverted to my crotch."

Bella laughed softly, but she wasn't surprised by his words. By his own admission, Wyatt was a ho-dog, and he often thought with his dick. Their active sex life was a great memory for her, and she was quite sure for him, too.

"I can have Hawk check on you every once in a while," Wyatt said.

"I'm going to be in a building full of people," she said. "I might not have a new eight-foot fence around the building, like you do at the ranch, but I will tell everyone to be on the lookout for anything out of the ordinary. Frank took care of my horses today, but I have to get back on track tomorrow. I leave here at six in the morning."

"I start work on the ranch right after that," Wyatt said. "I'll leave when you do."

That was too easy, she knew. Something told her he would follow her out to Frank's, and make sure no one else was around."

"We have to get to the bottom of the threat," Wyatt said.

"I have a plan for that," Bella said. "It involves the paper and people's propensity to gossip."

"Fourteen-year-old gossip?" he asked.

"There's always a kernel of truth in gossip," she said. "The theft is already the talk of the town because Reed and Leslie found the artifacts. Once I write my column for Wednesday's paper it will grow. We'll figure it out from there."

"I like that you said we," he said. "I miss being a we with you."

So do I, she wanted to answer, but she didn't. There was no way she was going to be back with Wyatt. Her heart couldn't take the pain again.

"Listen, I know you had nothing to do with the theft, and I intend to let the town know that."

"Are you going to tell them we were fucking for the first time?" he asked.

"Not in so many words," she countered. "But I am going to tell people we were together."

"That will piss off the bitch from the museum, who has always blamed me," he said. "Would you like to interview me about that night? I could give you my memories, about how soft and sweet and warm you were."

She wasn't sure how to respond, because he'd never said anything like that to her before. It made her want to hold him close, to feel his lips on her body.

"I remember how nervous we both were," he said. "But that didn't stop us. When I was inside you for the first time I knew there was nowhere else I wanted to be."

"Right then," Bella said. "But you soon found other places, didn't you?" She hated her words, even though they were the truth. He was being so sweet, remembering things that made her body tingle, but she was slapping him in the face, bringing back bad memories.

"I'm going to go write my column for Wednesday," she said. "You can do whatever you want, as long as it doesn't include me."

She closed her bedroom door after her and leaned against it, trying as hard as she could not to think about the handsome cowboy who knew how to please her so well standing just feet away.

Bella's Musings
   By Bella Beaumont
   © *The Bookman Gazette*

No, you haven't slipped back in time fourteen years. For those of you who missed the disclaimer on the news story on page one about the theft of the artifacts from the museum fourteen years ago, let me assure you it hasn't happened again. But we are looking into the theft once more. The recovery of the items just weeks ago has sparked interest in the events.

Recent events have also sparked old rumors, well I suppose sparked is not the proper word—more like rekindled. Do you remember where you were when the thefts happened? It's one of those questions people ask themselves about a major event. I know where I was because I was with the love of my life. At least he could be called that fourteen years ago. Times change, and while Wyatt Coleman and I are no longer the love of each other's lives, I hate that people have blamed him for the theft. I can assure you he is not guilty. We were together when the theft occurred, and together when we heard about the theft the next day at the Rescue Ranch.

What I would like to ask from you, dear readers, is to think back to the night of the thefts. One of the reasons we reprinted the original article on page one was so people might put themselves back in time, figuratively. If you think about it and remember something that might identify the thieves.

If you come up with something new, please call The Bookman Gazette offices, or drop us an email. It is our goal to solve this crime, even though the items have been recovered.

Bella read over what she'd written. It was enough, hopefully, so people would stop talking about Wyatt. She didn't want to get too personal, and tell her readers that the night of the museum theft was the night she and Wyatt had taken each other's virginity.

She thought about adding information about a reward if information led to an arrest, but she wasn't sure that was a good idea. She needed to talk to others about it, maybe her mother and brothers if she were offering newspaper money. She hated the idea of not offering something, because even if people wanted to help and uncover the truth, they responded better to money.

Even though it was almost three in the morning, she reread her column, which was short and to the point. She wasn't tired, and it was hard to sleep with Wyatt in the other room.

Having her face so close to his crotch had excited her beyond belief. Her body was on fire, her nipples hard and tingly; and her clit… well it was pulsing as it used to in the years they were together.

Bella closed down her laptop and put it on the floor under

her bed. Then she opened the drawer of her bedside table, ready to reach for a vibrator to take care of the need pulsing through her. But if she did that Wyatt would hear. He would come and investigate. He would see he'd affected her much more than she was willing to admit.

That would put him in control, and although he'd been her Dom, and her Daddy, she didn't want to give him that power over her now.

She wanted sex, and her BOB wouldn't do it tonight, not when Wyatt was so close. She stalked to the door and threw it open.

"Get your ass in here," she said. "I need to fuck."

Chapter 7

Wyatt jumped up from the sofa and went to the bedroom as quickly as possible. He had hoped for this, but the fact she called for him shocked him to no end. It wasn't like Bella to change her mind, and her words earlier that evening about not thinking about his dick rang true to him. He'd thought about jacking himself off later, after she'd said she was going to the bedroom to work on her column for the week. But he didn't want her to hear him, and come out to find him with his cock in his hands.

Of course her calling for him would make her think she was in charge, too, and that wouldn't do. His Dom side had to come out now, because if it was one thing Bella liked it was rough sex, and he would give it to her tonight.

"You called for me?" he asked.

"Just get naked," she answered.

"You first," he responded. They both wanted to be in charge, but he was definitely going to take the lead. Just like old times. When she didn't move to do as he'd said he put his hand on her shoulder and pushed. She toppled onto the bed, her eyes wide.

Wyatt straddled her and pinned her arms above her head. "So you want to fuck, but you don't want to take your clothes off? One thing leads to another, you know."

"You're still dressed," she said.

"Are you talking back to me?" Wyatt asked.

"Simply pointing out a fact," she said.

Wyatt loved the tremor in her voice; it had always wobbled when she was excited.

"Shall I just rip them off?" He rather liked that idea, but Bella shook her head violently.

"Wyatt, this is hard for me," she said. "Can we please just do things normally?"

"Since when have we ever been normal?" The answer was obvious… never. But he didn't want to push things. This was, for all intents and purposes, make-up sex from so many years ago when he'd screwed things up between them. He let go of her arms and at the same time leaned over and kissed her, softly. Bella moaned and his cock, already hard and ready for action, pressed against his jeans as if begging for release. He moved his lips to the corner of her mouth, then to her neck.

Maybe she was right and he needed to be gentle with her. He nibbled on her gently, savoring the salty taste of her skin. He tugged the edge of her t-shirt down to expose her shoulder. She pushed him off and sat up enough to pull her shirt over her head. She then tossed it onto the floor. When she was on her back again, he kissed her shoulder once more, then trailed his lips down to the swell of her breasts.

He wanted her bra gone, too, and it took all his willpower not to rip it off.

As if she'd read his mind she giggled. "Don't you dare. Those things are expensive."

He continued to kiss and lick her skin, then ran the palm of his hand over her silky bra. Her nipples were hard under his touch, and he once again fought the urge to rip the fabric from her body.

"This needs to go," he said as he continued to stroke the material.

Bella mumbled something that he really didn't understand. But he took it as assent because she sat up as much as she could with him still straddling her. She reached behind her and the bra loosened. Wyatt took hold of the straps and eased them off her shoulders.

Bella giggled and then lay back down. She wiggled her hips, and Wyatt's cock pulsed with need. He reminded himself she wanted it 'normal', so he needed to behave himself tonight.

He put his hand on her shoulder and gently pushed, but instead of falling back down she thrust her hips up and Wyatt lost his balance. He toppled down next to her and she was on him in seconds. He tried to sit up, but Bella pushed him back down and was on him in seconds.

"I know I said normal, but this is going at a snail's pace, and it's driving me crazy and not in a good way." She thumped his chest with her fist. "But of course you're wearing far too many clothes for what I need. So stay where you're at."

"Are you telling me what to do?" Wyatt asked.

"Quite a change of events for us, isn't it?" she asked with a giggle. "But yes, I'm telling you what to do." She got up and went to the end of the bed. She tugged off his boots, first the right one, then the left. Next to go were his socks.

"Pew yew!" she said as she tossed them aside. "Looks like your feet still sweat in those nasty boots."

"Like yours don't," he said.

"Are you accusing me of having stinky feet?" she asked.

"Just throwing back the insult," he said.

"Maybe I should find someone else to take care of my needs," she said.

"Nobody can take care of your needs like I can," Wyatt answered. He'd missed this. Even though Bella was submissive she still gave back as good as he gave.

"Is what you give me different than what you give others?" she asked.

"Because I love you," he said. "Sometimes I let my dick think for me, and when that happens I do stupid shit. You know me better than anyone, so you should know that."

Bella stared down at him, and he felt the intensity of her gaze, even in the darkness.

"Shouldn't you say loved, as in past tense?" she asked.

"No," Wyatt answered. "It's not a spoken typo. I still love you, Bella. I'll always love you. I realize I killed your love for me—and that is past tense—and I'll kick myself in the ass for that for the rest of my life. But I do love you."

She put her hands on his chest, and for a moment he thought she was going to slap him. Instead she said, "I hate you."

"I realize that," he said. "I think we've lost the mojo."

"Not on your life," she said. "I need a hard dick, and you're giving it to me."

"Then let me sit up and get undressed," he said.

For a moment he thought she was going to stay put. But she stood up and started toward the bathroom.

"I'll be back," she called out over her shoulder. "Get naked."

"You, too," he said, but his only answer was the closing of the bathroom door.

———

Bella closed and locked both doors that led to the bathroom, the one from the bedroom and the one from the main part of the house. After she'd flipped on the light she looked at herself in the mirror. Her face was flush and tears hung at the corner of her eyes.

"Damn you Wyatt Coleman," she whispered. She could have made it through sex without hearing the words I love you. She knew Wyatt well enough to know he wasn't lying to her, and it tugged at her heart. The problem was, as Rosa had said the other night, Bella loved Wyatt, too, but she'd come to terms with the fact that they wouldn't be together.

Yet here they were, in her bedroom, about to have sex— and the jerk professed his love for her. Damn him. She wanted to slap the crap out of him. If her body would allow it she would kick him out of her bed and go without. But there was no way that was happening. She needed to fuck, or she would go nuts.

She just had to convince her heart it was nothing more than physical. "Hear that?" she asked herself. "No feelings involved, just sex and an orgasm. Or two. Hopefully two."

"Did you call someone, or are you talking to yourself?"

"Either way I came in here for privacy," she said. "Are you naked yet?"

"I'm hard, too, but I'm also getting old," he said. "I can't keep it up forever, you know."

"Something tells me you're just pushing my buttons," she said. Bella ran her fingers through her hair, then went to the door that led to the bedroom. She stopped before she turned the knob because she realized she was still half dressed.

"There's only a few buttons I want to press, and one of them is between your legs," he said. I've already pressed the other two. Now get out here."

"Bossy, bossy," she said, even though that's one of the things she loved about him. She quickly took off the rest of her clothes and once again reached for the doorknob. Try as she might, she wanted to believe this was just a one night thing. But that wasn't going to happen, she knew. Once she'd tasted Wyatt again there was no way she was going to be able to let go.

Something told her he knew that, too.

She opened the door and padded into the bedroom. Wyatt lay in the middle of the bed, his hands laced behind his head. He was naked, and his rock-hard cock lay against his body. Bella licked her lips in anticipation. She crossed the room and knelt on the side of the bed, lowering her head to take him in her mouth.

"Don't you believe you should have asked for permission first?" he said, his voice tight with need.

"If I was serving my Master, yes," she said after she lifted her head. "But remember this is only sex." She took him in her mouth once more, and ran her tongue around the head of his cock.

His groan of pleasure made her suck him harder.

"Careful," he said. "I thought you wanted to fuck."

She did, but she'd always loved giving head, and tasting him was sheer perfection. Rather than slowing down as he asked, she took more of him in her mouth and continued to torment the tip of him with her tongue.

When he started to buck his hips she let him drop from her mouth. She took his dick in her hand and pumped gently as she flicked her tongue over where his cock joined his balls. She flicked her tongue over the vein, because she knew how much he loved it, how it drove him crazy.

"Fuck me," he said.

"As you wish." Bella pumped him a few more times before she straddled him, placing herself right above his cock. As hard as it was to control herself, Bella let herself down slowly, taking his hardness inside her. Wyatt bucked his hips in her direction and Bella pulled back, determined to take this slowly.

"I'm in charge tonight," she said, her voice low and husky. "You have to take what I give and not try and take over."

"For tonight," Wyatt replied. "But the next time you'll fall back in line as you should and follow your Master's orders."

"That's awfully cocky of you to assume I'll call you Master again."

"I'm nothing if not sure of myself," Wyatt said. He grabbed her hips and held her in place as he thrust upwards. His cock hit the sweet spot inside her and Bella's body seized in delicious anticipation. He thrust once more and she came. She shivered and felt as if she might explode. Before she recovered he tumbled her over and was on top of her so fast her head spun. When he thrust back inside her he, amazingly enough, hit the same spot, which still pulsed from the first orgasm.

Pleasure swept through her with each thrust, and she closed her eyes and wondered why she hadn't forgiven him before now, so they could have been enjoying this for the last few years. Bella wrapped her legs around his hips as he rode her. She closed her eyes and relished the feel of him sliding in and out.

As he rode her, Bella couldn't help but think back to the past, of how they'd discovered different things together, either from learning from talks with friends, or from books they'd bought during trips to Amarillo or Dallas.

They knew each other so well, which was one of the reasons she'd wanted to take things slow today, so it wouldn't be something she wanted to happen again. But now that she knew she didn't want to give it up once more, she was ready for something hard, as he was doing right now.

He kept hitting just the right spot, and then suddenly he left her and pulled back and sat on his knees. He pulled her toward him until her buttocks were on his thighs. She missed the feel of his dick inside her, but when he grabbed her throbbing clit between his thumb and forefinger and squeezed she gasped.

Wyatt tightened his grip on her clit, and the pressure drove her over the edge. "Wyatt!" she screamed.

"Yes, my love?" He pinched her clit again and her body jerked.

"Who is in charge, Bella?" he asked.

Bella shook her head, not willing to say the words.

"Tell me," he said as he pinched her once more.

"You are," she said, through the haze of pain that was running through her.

"Let's go back to the cocky discussion of earlier," Wyatt said. "You're in charge...? How do you finish that?"

No, no, she didn't want to say that tonight. It was too soon.

"Say it," Wyatt said as he pinched her clit once more.

"And if I don't?" she asked.

"My belt's already off," Wyatt said. "Seems to me you like to be spanked, but using the belt can go a bit far for you. Shall we test that theory tonight? How long has it been since you've tasted leather? Would thirty, or forty swats make you say what I want?"

Bella stared up at him, unwilling to give up her advantage. After thinking about it for a few, long moments she said, "Fuck off. I hate you sometimes."

"You know what they say. There is a fine line between love and hate."

"I crossed that line years ago!" She got up and started to pace. She didn't want to tell him that she was going back and forth now, that she loved him one moment and hated him the next. "I'm not calling you Master anymore, or Daddy. You can forget that right now. The best thing for you to do is get the fuck out of my bedroom."

"Your mouth is going to add to your swats."

Bella balled up her fists and screamed, "Get! The! Fuck! Out!" She unfurled a fist long enough to point a finger at her bedroom door. "Get! The! Fuck! Out!" she screamed at the top of her lungs. If someone was downstairs they would have heard her and probably called the sheriff's department. But she didn't care. She wasn't going to allow herself to fall under Wyatt's spell again. It would be too painful, and not in the leather meets ass way.

When he didn't move she stared at him, then said in a normal tone of voice. "Please, leave."

This time he nodded and went back to the living room.

It took all her self-control not to give in to the love side and call him back.

Chapter 8

"The phone is ringing off the hook, and the paper is not out until Wednesday. It's Monday. You just had to offer a reward, didn't you?"

Bella looked up from the paperwork on her desk to where Lily Blackwell stood in the doorway to her office. As the office manager at the Gazette, Lily tracked everything that happened in the office.

"The pages are in markup, which means anyone who works here could have read them," Bella said. "Someone opened their big mouth and told someone else, who told someone else. Have the callers had any information?"

"Are you kidding me?" Lily said. "Nobody has any real information on what happened fourteen years ago."

"Somebody does," Bella said.

"What everybody knows about is you being kidnapped from Rowdy's Saturday night by Wyatt Coleman."

Bella tightened her grip on the pen in her hand.

"Several callers said you were offering a reward to find someone else to shift the blame onto," Lily said. "Most of the town thinks Wyatt is guilty. And lots of people are saying a ranch truck was parked outside your house last night. All night."

"Damn gossips," Bella said.

"That's ironic, isn't it?" Lily asked. "You're asking for gossip from over ten years ago, and you're complaining that people are talking about something that happened Saturday."

"Whose side are you on?" Bella asked her. "Besides, I'm not looking for gossip, I'm asking for facts about what people remember from the museum thefts."

"Gossip," Lily said. "After fourteen years it's not facts. Give it up, Bella, you'll never find out who did it."

"They solve cold cases," Bella said. "I'll figure it out."

"So you say."

Bella's phone buzzed and she picked it up.

Wyatt: *You tell me if you leave the building.*

"Damn text messaging," Bella said. "You can't scream at someone over text."

"Caps lock," Lily said. "Send your text in all caps, and that person will know you're yelling at them."

Bella unlocked her phone and called up the text. She put on caps lock and typed: *FUCK YOU.*

Seconds later her phone buzzed again.

Wyatt: *Didn't we try that last night?*

Bella: *Try being the optimum word. Considering you screw every woman you come across you should be better at it than you were last night.*

Wyatt: *You had an orgasm, didn't you? Two if I'm not mistaken.*

Bella: *I faked it.*

Wyatt: *Liar.*

Bella put down her phone and looked toward the door. Lily was gone, and Bella couldn't really blame her. She shouldn't have been paying so much attention to the phone while Lily was there. It was rude. Very rude.

But, truth be told, Wyatt was the thing she needed to deal with right now. Last night had turned nasty so quickly. She should have given in to her desires and called him Master, but there was a part of her that just couldn't do it. No matter what she felt, she was still so upset about their break-up, and so afraid it would happen again if she let him in, that it just took over.

Truthfully, she would love to call him Master, and Daddy, again. But that opened her up for pain, and she wasn't sure she could handle it again.

Her phone dinged once more and she looked at the screen, ready to see something from Wyatt. Instead it was a text from Rosa.

Rosa: *Heard you got laid last night. Good for you.*

Rather than answering this one, Bella called her friend and said, "What the hell?"

"Everyone in town knows you and Wyatt spent the night together," Rosa answered. "And everyone knows what happened Saturday night, and that his truck is still parked at the bar. Everyone in town knows the two of you are sleeping together again. I commend you on taking my advice."

"Who told you all this?" Bella asked. "Who called you? Your mother? Your sister? Who else knows?"

"I told you, everyone knows. You and Wyatt are the talk of the town. Plus, I hear you're offering a five-hundred-dollar reward for information on the museum theft, as to the identity of the thief, or thieves, rather."

Bella mentally kicked herself in the butt for putting the reward into her column without talking to her brothers, or her mother. She wished she knew who had read the column and spread the news across town. Now that the information was out she couldn't change it. She needed to call Lily back and see if they needed to hire a few high school students to help answer the phones. And then to go through the information and see if there was anything useful.

Her phone vibrated in her hand and she ignored it. Since

she was talking to Rosa it was obviously Wyatt bugging her once more. What did he want this time? She regretted her decision to go and see him Saturday night. She should have gone to her brothers, or even Wyatt's brother, Hawk.

Seeking out Wyatt had opened a Pandora's Box for her, one that she didn't know how to close, or to live with. It would end up causing her more trouble, she was sure of that, because he would not back off. She never should have had sex with him last night. It had ended so badly, and there was no way he would give up. Damn him.

Her phone buzzed again, and Rosa said, "Are you listening to me?"

"No, I'm sorry, I can't concentrate this morning," Bella said.

"It was that good, huh?" Rosa asked with a laugh. "I'm jealous. All I got last night was a question about dinner and a request to make sure all his jeans were washed."

"Tell him you'll wash his jeans if he fucks you while the washer is on the spin cycle and you're sitting on top of it," Bella said. "You'll come hard."

"Or throw the washer off balance," Rosa said.

"It'll be worth it, trust me," Bella said.

Her phone buzzed again, and in her mind, Bella heard her father yelling at her to answer the phone. That's what the buzzer was, a parent telling her to pay attention. Wyatt could wait.

"I'll give it a try," Rosa said. "But it will have to be after the kids go to bed, and the noise of the washer might wake them up."

"Are you telling me you're super quiet every time you have sex?" Bella asked. "No wonder you're asking about my sex life."

"You have three kids and see how you do," Rosa said.

A knock at the door caught Bella's attention. "Your

brother is on the phone," Lily said. "And the museum lady is in the office, and she looks pissed."

"Abby?" Bella asked. "Give me a few moments with my brother—which one is it?"

"Frank," Lily said, "and he sounds pissed, too."

Bella pulled her phone away from her ear and pulled down the notifications. There was Frank's name on the text notifications with the letters *WTF*.

"I gotta go," Bella said to Rosa.

"Call me tonight," Rosa said, and the line went silent.

"Frank first," Bella said to Lily. "Abby can wait."

She picked up the landline on her desk and said, "Good morning, Frank."

"What the fuck?" her brother said. "A five-hundred-dollar reward. Have you lost your fricking mind? Mom is livid."

"And she sent you to do her dirty work? Typical."

"She says you're wasting newspaper money," Frank said. "And I agree."

"I'll pay it out of my own pocket," Bella said. "I want the truth, and money talks."

"People lie for money," Frank said. "Scrub it before it goes to print."

"No," Bella said. "Too many people know about it already." She really needed to talk to her staff about spreading newspaper information before publication day.

"Pull it, Bella," Frank said. "It was fourteen years ago. Forget it. Just drop it."

"You're repeating yourself, Frank," Bella said. "Forget it and drop it mean the same thing. And to repeat myself I say no, I'm not dropping it. I was given full editorial control of the newspaper. You don't get a say on what I do here, except financially. And like I said, I'll use my own money for the reward."

"You listen to me," Frank said.

But before he could continue, Bella said, "I have an appointment here, so I'm not going to listen to you. I've said my piece. Goodbye Frank."

"Bella, don't you hang up on me!"

Bella did just that. At the same time her cell phone buzzed. It was another text, this one from Wyatt.

Wyatt: *I'll bring lunch around one.*

Bella: *Don't bother.*

Wyatt: *Homemade by Austin.*

That was almost enough to make her change her mind. But she didn't respond. She could be bribed with food, but she wasn't sure now was the time.

She placed her cell on the desk and picked up the landline and punched the number for Lily's desk. When the office manager picked up, Bella said, "Send Abby back, but if Wyatt shows up, send him away."

"Yeah, like he's going to listen to me," Lily said. "Abby, you can go on back."

Bella imagined Abby sitting in the chair near Lily's desk, waiting impatiently. Abby might be an old lady, but she was not a sweet old lady by any means. She saw the museum as her personal domain and Abby and her family had donated most of the money to open the museum.

Bella stayed behind her desk. It was best to keep a buffer zone between herself and Abby. The moment Abby appeared, Bella knew she'd made the right move, because the look on Abby's face showed she was loaded for bear.

"What can I do for you, Abby?" Bella asked.

"You can write me a check for five-hundred-dollars, because I know, and have always known, who stole the artifacts. Your lover, Wyatt Coleman."

Bella shook her head. "This again? Obviously, you've heard about the reward from someone who released information early." She really had to talk to her staff. "But you haven't read the whole column. I was with Wyatt the night of the thefts. He didn't do it."

"Lying for him, as always," Abby said. "I'm prepared to make a statement that I saw him—with my own eyes.

"Who is lying now?" Bella asked. "I've read the sheriff's department reports from that time, and you specifically said someone—you didn't see who—broke into the museum and took the items. So were you lying then? Or now?"

"I saw him," Abby said.

"I'll be sure to let the sheriff's office know you lied back then." Bella shrugged. "And my parents always told me if someone would lie to you once, you could not trust anything they ever told you."

Abby looked ready to vault across the desk and attack Bella.

"I'm not sure why you hate Wyatt so much, but I am willing to swear on the Bible he did not steal the relics."

"My word against yours, then," Abby said.

"And since your words prove you lied fourteen years ago, I think they'll believe me." Bella picked up the phone. "Shall we give it a go?"

Bella stared at the museum director, who was focused on the phone.

"Shall I dial the sheriff's department, or should I put the phone down since you're lying to me?"

For a moment, Bella thought Abby would call her bluff. Instead, the woman moved into the office and sat down in one of the chairs.

"While you're here, why don't you tell me exactly what was taken that night."

"A spear, pottery shards, and some arrowheads," Abby said.

"Nothing else?" Bella thought about the note, about how it

named the items that had been returned to the tribe, but how it wanted the one item back.

"Nothing else," Abby said.

"Since I know you're so good at lying, I have to tell you I don't believe you." Bella put her hands on her desk and leaned forward. "I have it on good authority something else was stolen, a piece of jewelry perhaps?"

Abby's mouth dropped open in shock, and Bella knew she wasn't the author of the note. The way Bella read Abby's expression, there was a necklace, but Abby didn't think anyone else knew about it, because she had not told the authorities about it at the time.

"What does it look like?" Bella asked.

"I have no clue what you're talking about." Abby turned her gaze toward the door, and at just that moment Wyatt stepped inside. Bella had been so focused on her visitor she hadn't heard any noise, but as he moved into the room, the jingling of his spurs caught her attention. He had a large paper bag in his hand and there was a wonderful smell filling the room.

"Well, well, if it isn't the head of the Bookman Springs' welcoming committee," Wyatt said. "Are you here seeking volunteers to welcome people to town, or are you delivering your new threat in person?"

"Threat?" Abby stood up and pointed a finger in Wyatt's direction. "You're a juvenile delinquent who grew into a horrible adult. What she sees in you is beyond everyone's imagination. But I've never threatened her, or you."

"Someone else knows about the necklace," Bella said. "If you never mentioned it to the sheriff's department, who did you tell?"

"I don't know what you're talking about," Abby said. "I know nothing about a necklace."

Bella glanced at Wyatt, who shook his head. He put the

bag on her desk and clasped his hands behind his back, as if he were trying to keep control of himself and not lash out at Abby.

"The relics stayed buried for fourteen years because of lies," Bella said. "Whoever took them still has the necklace. Who is it?"

"Your father buried them, so he would have known all about them," Abby said. "If there was a necklace, maybe he stole it, too."

"My father is dead," Bella said.

"All I'm saying is all roads lead to your family, or your lover," Abby said. "I was the victim in all this, not the thief."

She stormed out of the room, faster than Bella thought possible. When she was gone, Bella turned to Wyatt. "I don't remember issuing an invitation to you. Get out."

"Good to see you too," Wyatt answered. "I've got chicken salad sandwiches and potato salad."

"Please leave," Bella said. She had too much to deal with work wise, the last thing she needed was for Wyatt to exert control over her.

"I'm not leaving," Wyatt said. "So sit down, eat a sandwich, and tell me what she was doing here and what's been going on this morning."

She didn't want to argue, and she hadn't eaten breakfast that morning. The smell was too tempting.

"My stomach is telling me to eat, not you," Bella said.

Wyatt crossed to the door and closed it. "Let's eat, and then we'll have a chat," he said.

Chapter 9

Wyatt had polished off his third sandwich by the time Bella had started her first. She was trying to be sweet and tidy, eating in little bites. He wasn't sure if she was trying to prolong lunch because she knew he was going to lay down the law, or because she wasn't that hungry.

But he didn't see how the latter could be true if this was her first meal of the day. He'd had breakfast at the ranch, then told Austin he needed to take Bella food so she didn't expose herself by leaving the newspaper office.

He wasn't sure where his little brother found the recipe he'd used to make this salad, but it was delicious.

"If you don't hurry up I'm going to eat them all," Wyatt said.

"I can't imagine how you don't weigh three hundred pounds," she said.

"Metabolism, and lots of physical labor," Wyatt said. "Speaking of which I have a busy afternoon. I have to help Reed and Kyle float teeth on three new arrivals today."

"Fun," Bella said.

"You know, you can always board your horses at the ranch," he said. "I'd love to take care of them for you."

"Pass," Bella said. "They're fine at Frank's stables."

Wyatt nodded. It was too much to hope that she would have taken him up on the offer.

"Your choice," he said. "Now, we need to talk."

"You mean you need to talk," Bella said. "There's a difference."

"Then just listen," Wyatt answered. "We have a situation we have to face, and I'm not going to allow you to go your own way on it. If something happened and you died, I would not be able to live with myself. So I'm reinserting myself in your life as your Daddy, and your Dom."

"You can't do that," Bella said.

"I can, and I just did." Wyatt took a drink from the bottle of water he'd brought with him. After he'd swallowed he said, "I'm not going to waste time arguing with you about it. I'm taking charge. That's final."

"You dirty little…"

Wyatt slammed his hand on the desk. "Don't finish that sentence." He held up a finger and looked toward the door. Would someone come to investigate the noise? If they did, what would he say? That he'd knocked something over? He should have waited until after the newspaper was closed. But it was too late. Fortunately, the door did not open, but he knew the whole town was talking about him staying the night at Bella's last night. This would give them one more thing to gossip about.

"I take your silence as acceptance of my terms," Wyatt said.

"Terms? You mean the fact you're going to force me to accept you as Daddy and Dom?"

"It's not as if you've never done it before," Wyatt said.

"We have some serious problems to face here, and fighting about this issue takes time away from what we're facing."

"Sure, sure," Bella said. "Shall I clean off the desk so you can fuck me here and now, show your dominance over me? I'm sure you're frustrated because you didn't get a chance to finish last night."

"Watch your mouth," Wyatt said.

"Yes, Sir," she said as she saluted him. "I'll behave. Maybe."

"So nothing's changed." Wyatt took another drink of water. He expected more flash from her. It wasn't like her to just say, "I'll behave." He was sure, in her mind, she was already planning something that would cause him grief. As much as he had loved being her Daddy, and her Dom, in the past, they had other things they needed to think about now.

"What did the Mistress of Bitches want?"

"What everyone wants—money." Bella picked up a second sandwich, which he was glad to see. "She was prepared to give you up, swear that she saw you steal the stuff."

"Bitch," he said.

"When I let her know I knew she was lying she changed her tune." She took a small bite and a moan escaped her lips.

"How'd she find out about the reward?"

"I obviously have someone with a big mouth on staff," Bella said. "They read the proofs, and told someone, who told someone, who told someone."

"Ah, a gossip chain," he said.

"Lilly said the phone has been ringing off the hook." She shrugged, and took another bite. While she chewed, Wyatt wondered what she was thinking. After she swallowed she said, "Frank called, too, demanding that I take out the reward part. He says Mom is pissed."

"Weird," Wyatt said. "Don't you think she would want to

get to the truth? Seems to me it would clear your father's name totally if we find out whodunit."

"Yeah, I thought so too," Bella said. "And the fact she attacked me yesterday, well, it's just so odd. I mean, she's always been worried about her reputation, but she was ticked about Dad leaving a road map to the artifacts. She said it made him look like the thief. If we can prove he's not, she should be happy. So why is she so mad about all this?"

Wyatt had an idea, but he wasn't sure it was something Bella wanted to hear.

"She knows something," Bella said. "I refuse to believe Dad had this information and never shared it with her in the last fourteen years. I need to go talk to her."

"We can go tonight," Wyatt said.

To his surprise, Bella nodded. "I'll let her know we're coming. She doesn't like drop-ins."

"After dinner?" he asked. "Austin is expecting you to eat with us. He's making fried chicken."

"Chicken day at the ranch?" she asked before she took another bite of her sandwich.

"Must have been a sale at the supermarket." Wyatt winked at her and finished off his sandwich. He'd eaten far too many of them. "I've got to go. I'm meeting Reed and Kyle at the ranch in half an hour."

"I need to talk to Abby again," she said. "I'm pretty sure she knows more about the necklace. You should have seen the shock on her face when I mentioned it. That's what makes me think she didn't write the letter. She didn't want people to know about the necklace."

"Maybe," Wyatt said.

"I'm going to talk to Leslie, see if I can re-watch the video Dad made for Reed that led them to the artifacts."

"She's at their house now," Wyatt said. "She's meeting

with a contractor this afternoon about adding a room to the house."

"Thanks," Bella said. "If I drive to the ranch on my own am I going to be breaking Daddy's rules?"

"Daddy is determined to keep you safe," Wyatt said. "Text me when you're coming and I'll meet you at the gate."

Bella chuckled. "Hopefully that huge fence you're building will keep me safe once I get there."

"I'll keep you safe," Wyatt said.

"We'll see," Bella said.

Wyatt was certain she wasn't talking about physically safe.

Bella was tempted to transfer the video Leslie had just sent her to her office computer, but she was still unsure who had read her column early and given the information to almost all of Bookman Springs. So she kept it on her phone and hit play.

A lump formed in her throat as her Father's face appeared on the screen. When he started to talk, she felt tears form in her eyes. She fought them back as he talked about the relics, and how he'd taken them from young men he'd taught to keep them from getting into trouble and ruining their futures. He didn't say who they were, only where he'd hidden the items and how Reed, Wyatt's brother, could find them and get them back where they belonged.

Her mother had been furious with the whole situation, that her father had been more concerned with a young man's future than the reputation of his family. She'd been even angrier when Reed and his now wife, Leslie, had found the relics and returned them to the tribe they'd been taken from before they were given to the museum.

Seeing this again, and thinking of her mother's reaction to it, made Bella rethink her trip to her mother's house tonight.

Taking Wyatt with her might not be a good idea. Her mother had never really liked Wyatt. She'd considered him a bad influence on her daughter, and when Bella had broken ties with him, her mother had been thrilled. Something told her that taking Wyatt with her tonight would keep her Mother from talking. The best way to get information would be to go by herself.

Wyatt would be pissed, but she would deal with him later. Her mother would be more talkative if Bella was alone, or so she hoped.

She went out the back door, to avoid being seen on Main Street, or by anyone who might call Wyatt and tell him she was leaving. She hated to think there was someone who might turn her in, but she didn't think anyone would let information out early, either.

She climbed into her SUV and headed out of the alley. As per usual there was no traffic. The people of Bookman Springs were either at work, or at home. She turned right, then headed toward the highway that would take her to her mother's house. Bella was still unhappy with her brother Frank about his call that morning.

It was hard being the only girl in the family. Everyone wanted to control her, to tell her what to do. The only person she wanted to take instructions from was Wyatt, who had told her today that she would be doing exactly that.

She was thrilled he'd taken charge, but she also wished he'd done it last night when she'd been such a brat. But then again maybe he'd punish her for it tonight. That thought made her nipples tingle. It was hard to want something so intensely when you knew it would end up in disaster.

It was a beautiful summer day, and since she was usually stuck in the office during these days, Bella decided to take advantage of her freedom. She cut off the air conditioner and rolled down the front windows, giving her two-sixty air as her father used to call it—two windows down at sixty miles an hour.

She'd left her hair down that morning and it whipped around her face, and it made her feel free. She hated working in the office sometimes, devoting too much of her time to the newspaper. Life would be better if she had more time to ride her horse and well, just smile. The addition of a man in her life would be great, too. But not Wyatt. Toward the end of their relationship he brought more frowns than smiles. Too bad it wouldn't be any different now, because a thrill had run through her today when he'd told her he was going to be her Daddy/Dom and she was going to go along with it, no matter what.

She cranked up the sound on the radio, loving the oldies that always made her smile. Her father had listened to them, and she'd learned the words to most of them. She started to sing. After seeing her mother she might just go to Frank's and go for a ride rather than go back to the office.

Which reminded her, she needed to let Lily know she was not in her office. It wasn't fair to leave her office manager wondering where Bella was in case something important came up. She put her finger on the phone button on her steering wheel, but before she could instruct the phone to call the newspaper, it rang and the electronic voice announced Wyatt Coleman was calling.

She hit accept and Wyatt's voice filled the car. "Where are you going?" he asked in a singsong voice.

"You paying someone to follow me?" she asked.

"Hawk saw you heading out of town," he replied. "So I'll ask again, where are you going?"

"To Mom's," she said. "She'll talk better to just me."

"Sure," he said, and then he laughed. "You keep thinking that, and it might actually come true. Text me when you leave."

"Okay, Daddy," she said.

"Watch your tone, young lady," he said.

"Whatever." She disconnected the call, knowing full well she'd pay for it later. Then she called Lily and told her she'd left the office.

"Why am I not surprised?" Lily said. "The phone is still ringing off the hook with people wanting to know how they can collect their five-hundred-dollars."

"There are instructions in the column about how to submit tips. We need to change the phone number to a specific line, and then we need to hire a few high school kids to answer the phones. For now, remind people the paper doesn't come out until Wednesday, and that's when the phone lines open."

"Will do, Boss," Lily said. "May I ask where you're going?"

"To visit my mother." Bella thought about it for a few moments. She wanted to stay out, to have a fun afternoon, but things needed to be done to get the paper ready for publication. "I'll be back in an hour or so."

"See you then," Lily said.

Bella pulled onto the road that led to her mother's house. As she drew nearer she could see her brother Sam's truck parked outside. Sam reminded her the most of their father. He always thought about others first, and how he could help them.

She parked next to him, then went to the front door. Even though she'd grown up in this house she still knocked before entering. Her mother was not big on unannounced visitors. She waited at the door until Sam showed up on the other side.

"You're walking into a hornet's nest," Sam said. "You should go back to town."

"Thanks for the warning," she said. She turned her head at the sound of an approaching vehicle and then cursed under her breath when she saw a Rescue Ranch truck park behind her SUV. He must have been on the road when he'd called her.

"And the hornet's nest just doubled in size," Sam said with a chuckle. He raised his hand in greeting. "Wyatt, how's it going, buddy?"

"Perfect," Wyatt said. "And you?"

"Ready to enjoy the show," Sam said.

Her mother's voice rang out behind Sam.

"Who is it?" she asked.

"It's Bella, and Wyatt," Sam answered.

"Just perfect," her mother said, her tone belying her words. But then she said, "This could work. We can solve this situation here and now. Tell them to get in here."

Bella was tempted to scream out, "Not on your life," but then she remembered she'd come out to talk to her mother. The fact that Wyatt was here would add to the tension, but it also might make her mother let slip any information she had because her hackles were up.

Maybe having Wyatt here would work after all.

Chapter 10

"This should be fun," Wyatt said as he came up behind her. Bella fought the urge to turn around and pop him in the mouth.

"You couldn't let me do this on my own, could you?"

"Then I'd be falling down on the job," he said. "As it is I had to choose between my Daddy duties, and my work on the ranch. You should be thrilled I'm following my obligations to you."

"Screw you," she said.

"You two want to come in and fight, or just keep bickering on the front porch?" Sam asked.

Bella winced. She wondered how much her bother had heard, and if he understood what Wyatt meant when he mentioned his 'Daddy duties'. They hadn't been talking very loudly, but still, there was a chance he'd heard. She opened the screen door and stepped around Sam, who still stood in the doorway.

She turned to see Wyatt and Sam shaking hands. "How are things going at the ranch?" Sam asked.

"Floating teeth this afternoon, and I'm shirking my

responsibilities," Wyatt said. "Good thing I have two brothers who are vets."

"Floating is not a fun job," Sam said.

"Quit chatting and get in here," her mother called from the other room.

"This should be fun," Bella said as she headed toward what her mother called her sitting room. Bitsy Beaumont sat ramrod straight in a wingback chair. There was a silver coffee pot and two cups on the table in front of her. There was also a plate of breakfast pastries, although it was after one in the afternoon. Her mother had a sweet tooth, although you'd never know it to look at her. She was skinny as a rail.

"I've sent Connie for more cups," Bitsy said. "She'll be right back. Take a seat."

Poor Connie, Bella thought. The woman had been her mother's maid for as long as Bella could remember, and she didn't receive the best of treatment.

"So you two are back together?" Bitsy asked. "I'm glad your father is not alive to see this. He never liked you, Wyatt."

"Mother," Bella said. "Do you have to be so rude?"

"Honesty is not rudeness," Bitsy said. "Frank tells me you're refusing to remove that horrible column. I'm glad you're here then, because I am ordering you to do it. Now."

"I have complete editorial control at the paper," Bella said. "I print what I want. And what I want is the truth about the theft."

"Leave it alone, Bella," Bitsy said.

"Bella has a point," Sam said. "There are a lot of people in town who think Dad did it since he knew where to find the goods."

"I should have known you'd side with her," Bitsy said. "I am the head of this family now, and what I say goes. Cut it, Bella, or I'll fire you."

"You don't have the authority to fire me, Mother," Bella said.

"The boys will side with me," Bitsy said.

"Not all of us," Sam said.

"I am the head of this family!" her mother's voice rang out, and Connie stepped into the room, carrying a tray with cups. Bella had a feeling the woman had been standing just on the other side of the door, listening to the conversation.

Could Connie be the blabbermouth? If someone on her staff had told Frank, who had then told their mother, and Connie had overheard, she could be the leak. It wasn't that much of a stretch, Bella thought.

"You will do as I say," Bitsy said.

"Not likely," Sam said with a chuckle. "If Wyatt can't keep her in check, what makes you think you can?"

"Don't talk to me like that," Bitsy said.

"What are you hiding, Mother?" Bella asked. "Why are you so against what I'm doing?"

"Don't you dare question me," Bitsy said. "You will obey my orders."

Her mother's voice was low, and full of anger.

"I had hoped you would give me an idea about what you know," Bella said. "I can't believe you didn't know Dad had the relics."

Her mother stood and smoothed her hands down her jeans. "You can leave now. If I see your column in Wednesday's paper don't bother to come back."

Tears stung Bella's eyes, but she fought them back. She knew her mother meant it. Was she determined to lose her mother just weeks after her father's death?

"Mother, don't be ridiculous," Sam said.

"She's more worried about her reputation than about me, Sam," Bella said. "She knows something that she's not willing to share, and she's afraid someone will tell me."

"You can show yourself out," Bitsy said. She left the room, and Bella stared after her. She was happy Wyatt had stayed silent during the exchange.

"That was awkward," Wyatt said.

"Mother is still angry at Dad for hiding the relics all these years," Bella said.

"She's mad that people know and are talking about it," Sam said. "She's always been worried about her reputation."

"She knows something," Bella said. "I know I keep repeating that, but I know it has to be true." And it hurt, deep down inside. Her mother always thought about herself first. It had been hard growing up to have such different parents. Her father would have done anything for his family, and for his friends. But her mother... well, that was a totally different story. If she wanted someone to spend the night, or come over for dinner, she had to make sure she made plans at least two weeks in advance. If her father overrode her mother's decision and let her have friends over, Bitsy would be mad for days. She was not an easy woman to live with.

"You know what this means, Sam," Bella said.

"Yeah, I do," he said. "Either Dad, Frank, or Jesse, is our thief."

Her phone rang the moment Bella climbed back in her SUV.

"You don't really believe your dad took the relics," Wyatt said.

"Dad, no." She took a deep breath. "But Frank, maybe. I haven't talked to Jesse in days, but I don't think he would have done it. He wasn't calling me to get off the story, but Frank was, and he was as insistent as Mom was just now. I think Frank and his friends could have done it. And Dad would have covered it up for him, because Mom would have forced him to."

Are you okay?" Wyatt asked.

"No." Her voice broke as she spoke. She sniffled and took a napkin off the passenger seat to wipe her eyes. "Frank's right, I've poked a hornet's nest, and my family is going to get stung."

"The note writer poked the nest," Wyatt said. "And that is neither your mother, nor Frank. They wouldn't want to call attention to the situation. Someone is pissed the necklace was not among the recovered items. My guess is it's the queen of bitches, no matter what she said this morning."

Bella didn't answer him, but she was pretty sure he was right. "I have to go back to work."

"Dinner is at seven," Wyatt said. "I'll come get you around six-thirty."

"I'll try to be done by then," she said. "I have to get pages done and downloaded to our account in Lubbock so the paper can get printed tomorrow night. I haven't done enough today."

"Then get busy," he said with a laugh. The phone was silent for a few moments. "Are you okay?"

"Haven't we been over this?" She sniffled once more. "I don't think I'm going to be good company for dinner tonight."

"Having dinner with my family will brighten your mood," Wyatt said. "I'll see you around six-thirty."

Wyatt parked in back of the newspaper office and got out of his truck. It had been parked outside of Rowdy's until that afternoon, and he was glad to have it back. He put his hand on the hood of Bella's SUV. It was cold to the touch. He knew from Lily that Bella had been inside all afternoon, working on Wednesday's edition of the paper.

He reached for the door handle, but his phone dinged before he could open it.

The text was from Bella, who announced she was in her apartment. He headed up the stairs and found the door open. Bella was on the couch, her back to the door.

"It's been a bad day for you," he said.

"It has," she answered. "But on the work front we got a lot done this afternoon. And I pulled my column."

"That doesn't sound like you," he said.

"Why offer a reward when I know who did it?"

"So you pulled the whole thing?" he asked. "Why?"

"I guess pull isn't the right word." Bella turned toward him. "I rewrote it and took out the part about the reward."

"Did you blame your mother and brother?" he asked.

"Nope." She turned away from him. Her voice wobbled on the word, and when she'd been turned toward him he'd seen red eyes. She'd been crying.

He crossed the room and sat down next to her. When he wrapped his arm around her shoulders she leaned into him and started bawling.

"It's going to be okay, baby," he said. "I promise."

Her sobs intensified and he pulled her closer. She placed her head on his shoulder and said, "I've torn my family apart."

"Really?" Wyatt ran his hand up and down her arm. "That's like a murderer saying the victim made him kill her, or him. Don't blame yourself for what they did."

"Frank called," she said in between sobs. "He accused me of battering Mom this morning, of screaming at her and accusing her of being a thief. He told me I was no longer part of my family. He said I needed to move out of town."

Her words had come out between her sobs. Wyatt felt

anger like he hadn't experienced in years. He wanted to find Frank Beaumont and beat the ever-loving shit out of him. Instead he stayed where he was and tightened his hold on Bella.

"You have me," he said. "And my family is looking forward to having you for dinner tonight."

"They're going to eat me for dinner?" she asked with a laugh, and then she snorted and reached for a tissue that was on the coffee table. "You mean having me over."

"Even when you're upset you're correcting my grammar," he said.

"That's my goal in life," she said, "to correct your speech."

"Then you're doing it." Wyatt kissed her forehead. "Let's go before we're late. I'm hungry."

"Did you tell them what I figured out today?" she asked.

"No, we need dinner conversation," he said. "Plus, I wasn't sure you wanted to let it out yet."

"Maybe not," she said. "But I know they are going to ask."

"I'll take care of it," Wyatt said. He pulled his phone out of his pocket. He hit a few keys and told Hawk to tell everyone talk about the relics was off limits.

Hawk's answer was for them to hurry and get there so they could eat.

Bella went to wash her face, and when she was back he saw no traces of her sorrow on her face.

She stopped in the middle of the dining room where her purse sat on the table.

"Can we play when we get back?" she asked. "I need some downtime."

"Leave it to me," Wyatt said. "But I want you to read me the new column while I drive. I want to hear what you wrote."

He'd thought about this after she'd mentioned the rewrite. He wanted dinner to be fun, and since she wanted to play after he didn't want to mention what had happened today. But he wanted to know what she'd changed.

Bella's Musings
  By Bella Beaumont
  © The Bookman Gazette

If there is one thing I've always hated to hear it's the phrase, "Life turns on a dime."

I never really understood it when I was younger. I know now what it means, but until today I guess I never really thought it would happen to me. My father died suddenly, as everyone knows. But that is not life turning on a dime. Dad was one of those 'Live each day like it's your last' type of guys. That means we always said I love you, and we never put off to tomorrow what could be done today.

Monday started out perfect. I knew what I wanted to write for my Wednesday column, but then it changed on, as you can imagine, the turn of a dime.

Someone who shall remain nameless is back in my life, as you can imagine, on the turn of a dime.

So my life turned on Monday. It might turn again on Tuesday, but by then the paper will have been put to bed, and you won't hear about it. Or will you? One of the things I figured out on Monday is the old saying 'News spreads like wildfire', is true, even before it hits the printer.

Some of you know I'm interested in finding out what happened fourteen years ago when the museum lost some of its items by way of theft. I had originally thought of offering a reward for information. But I've changed my mind. I hope if someone knows what happened fourteen years ago they would tell me because it is the right thing to do, not because someone offered them money.

That means I'm putting it out there right now. If you remember anything that might help identify the culprits in the museum thefts, please call the newspaper office and give us the information. If we find out who stole the items, even if it's too late to prosecute them, it will be good to finally know the truth.

Don't think of giving information as gossiping. We need to get to the truth, to finally put the matter to rest. If you can help do that, I look forward to hearing from you.

Chapter 11

"You do realize you've just told the entire town we're back together?"

"I think I did it to piss off my mother," she said. "She was lying when she said Dad didn't like you. He told me once you were a good man, and I needed to give you a second chance."

Wyatt wanted to believe her. Coach had always been good to him, even though he was different than his brothers. He didn't play sports, he didn't give a damn what people thought about him, and he broke rules and got into trouble—a lot. Which was why people like the queen of bitches blamed him for everything.

The best thing that had happened in his life was Bella, and he'd screwed that up, too. Hopefully, he could get it back on track now, and keep it going.

"I wish you'd done it for yourself," he said. He pulled off the highway and stopped at the ranch gate. He pressed the button to open it and while he waited he tried not to stare at her. How many times had they come to the ranch while they were together before? Unlike Bella's mother, his parents were open and welcoming and Bella ate with them a great deal of the time. Afterward they would take a ride, where they would lay out under a tree and have great sex.

Bella had said she'd wanted to play afterward, and he thought recreating one of those nights would be perfect. He wondered if she remembered those nights, and if they fueled her fantasies as they did his.

She was definitely taking his 'you're mine again' speech better than he'd thought she would. He hoped that was a good sign.

He piloted the truck through the gate and stopped inside to close it.

"The Great Wall of Coleman is going up fast," Bella said. "What was the reason for it again?"

Wyatt chuckled. He couldn't remember what he'd told her the first time she'd asked, so he just said, "That sounds like a question a journalist would ask to trip someone up." He thought about it for a moment and then continued, "We had a break-in, and we're just trying to make it harder on someone wanting to help themselves."

"Right," she said. "I thought y'all had a few big dogs, too."

"We do, but they spend most of their time by the stables." He pulled up in front of the house and parked next to Hawk's truck.

"I remember giving you head in this exact spot," Bella said.

His cock hardened immediately at the memory. He could feel her mouth on him, her tongue teasing the head like she did so expertly. "Fuck, Bella, don't say things like that before we have to go in front of all of my family." He put his hand on his crotch and pressed down. He didn't want to go in the house with a hard-on. One of his brothers would notice and they'd be sure to mention it, and laugh about it.

"I'm sorry," she said, sarcastically. "What can I do to make it better?" She licked her lips, and Wyatt wanted to take her over his lap and spank the ever-living daylights out of her.

"Fucking behave," he said.

"Um, fucking no?" She smiled. "Like you, I've never behaved, so I don't know why I should start now."

"Because I'm ordering you to," Wyatt answered.

"Yeah, that hasn't worked in the past, has it?" She batted her eyes at him.

"Then let's try it this way," Wyatt said. "Behave, or I swear to God I'll spank you in front of everyone."

"Promise?"

She put her hand on his dick and it hardened even more. Dinner was going to be miserable.

"Screw around later!" Hawk's voice rang out from the front of the house. "We're starving and tired of waiting on you."

"Shall we eat?" She stuck out her tongue and wiggled it around, and her meaning was clear.

"Damn you, Bella," he said. "You're being a brat."

"You'd be disappointed if I wasn't." She opened the door and got out. "Sorry, Hawk, my fault," she called out.

She started toward the door and was already on the porch when he was still getting out of the truck.

"Hurry up," Hawk called out again.

Wyatt walked to the porch as fast as he could, his dick pressing against his jeans. When he stepped up next to Bella he glared at her. She would pay for this later.

Bella put her hand on Wyatt's thigh and squeezed gently. Dinner was over, and it had gone well, with talk about the ranch and the horses they'd brought in just a few days ago. His cock was no longer hard, which was both good, and bad. She'd hoped he would stay that way until after dinner, but as he'd told her, he wasn't as young as he used to be.

She knew he would punish her for being a brat, but she wondered if he would punish her as her Daddy, or her Dom. She hoped it would be as her Dom. She would rather he kept the Daddy part until they were back at her apartment.

Bella felt angry with herself for taking him back so easily. At first she'd told herself it was just until they got to the bottom of the theft. But she'd figured out what was what, and here she was, sitting next to him at family dinner, hoping he would spank her later, or punish her in some sort of way that made her feel like his little once again.

It was a scary thought, because she'd never thought to open herself up to a man again, let alone Wyatt, even though he was the only man she had ever loved.

"Bella and I are going for a ride," Wyatt announced.

"Bella, you can ride my horse again if you want," Austin said.

"Thank you," Bella said.

"Take a blanket," Hawk said as they walked out of the room.

She was happy her back was to them so they couldn't see the blush that heated her cheeks. The brothers obviously knew she and Wyatt got frisky out on the ranch lands. She figured they did, too, with their ladies, so she shouldn't be embarrassed. But it was hard knowing they all knew what was happening.

The thought of what she'd written in her column, and what would soon be public knowledge, wiggled inside her. That was probably a mistake. It was true she'd done it to piss off her mother, or so she told herself. The truth was she'd missed Wyatt, and she was using her mother as an excuse.

Maybe she should change her column again, take out the part about renewing a relationship. It wasn't something that needed to be spread across town. But then again if she had a spy in her shop, that information was already spreading across town. And if that spy was affiliated with her mother, then the woman would be calling right now, screaming about Bella getting back with the reprobate.

She followed Wyatt to the back door where she watched as he picked up a pair of saddlebags. He offered her one and when she picked it up she though it was heavy for what she figured would be some cookies and a few bottles of water.

They walked to the stables and she saddled Austin's horse while Wyatt did his. She liked riding at night, especially when it was clear and they would get the chance to see stars. When the horses were saddled, she watched Wyatt attach a bundle to the back of his horse. She'd been out with him enough to know it wasn't a blanket, but a sleeping bag. She loved the idea of spending the night on the ranch. Things like this were some of the great things she and Wyatt had in common.

They mounted up and she took off first, heading her mount to the right.

"Wait!" Wyatt called out. "Not that way."

Bella pulled up on the reins. "Isn't that lake over there? That's where we always camped before. We can go skinny dipping in the moonlight."

"We just can't," he said.

"Why not?" she asked. When he didn't answer she said, "Wyatt, what's happened at the lake? Did something go wrong? Did you have to drain it?"

"No." He rode up next to her and then headed to the left. "We have a fire pit out here."

Bella started to follow his lead. When she was next to him she said, "What's up with the lake? Are y'all growing pot out there? Or cooking meth? I like that area and was looking forward to seeing it again."

"You'll like the new area we fixed up," Wyatt said. "It's really new, just a few months old. It has a fire pit, and a barbecue area. There are also picnic tables with covers, and a bathroom, so you don't have to squat and pee."

"I like that idea, but I don't understand why y'all gave up the lake area." She wanted a really good explanation, but something told her she wasn't going to get it. They rode for about half an hour, kicking the horses into a good gallop at one point. When Wyatt pulled up and pointed off to the left, Bella stopped and stared.

There was no lake, but there was a great camping area. It had all the items he'd described, and she had to admit it made her happy. "You need to add a lake," she said. "Skinny dipping is fun."

"I have some fun planned," Wyatt answered. They unpacked the supplies, and out of one saddlebag he pulled out what looked to her like hemp rope.

"You gonna spank my bottom with that?" she asked.

"Maybe in the morning," he said. "But tonight, I have something else in mind."

"You could spank me with it as a build-up to whatever you have planned," Bella said.

"Are you trying to top from the bottom?"

"Just offering a suggestion."

"One that I'm going to ignore," Wyatt said. "But you can strip now. I want you naked in one minute."

Bella crossed to the picnic table and sat down. She pulled off her boots, thankful to see a walking path between the table and the concrete slab where Wyatt was setting up the sleeping bags and pillows. She wondered how many of those items he'd carried here, and how many had been stored in the little unit that was next to the slab.

Which made her wonder how many times this place was used, and if Wyatt had brought anyone else out here. Which was one of the reasons why she'd wanted to go to the lake. He'd promised her once that he'd never take another woman out there, and she believed him.

"You sure are moving slow for a woman who was just given an order," Wyatt said. "Bare feet do not equal a naked body."

"I'm getting there," Bella said as she started to unbutton her shirt."

"You won't make it in time," Wyatt said. "And I think you're doing it on purpose."

"What makes you think I would ever do that." She shrugged off her shirt, then put her fingers on her bra's hooks. She undid them easily and then let her bra fall to the concrete.

"The longer you take, the more you wait," Wyatt said.

"Wait for what?" she asked.

"Wait for relief," he answered. "You seem to think sending me into dinner with a hard-on would have no consequences."

Bella stared at him, her heart thumping faster and faster. "I was just playing."

"You think?" He flicked the hemp in her direction. "Your minute is up and you're still dressed. That doesn't bode well for you."

"I'm sorry," she said. "I stepped over my bounds, and I'm really sorry."

"You will be," he said. "Why are you standing there, doing nothing?"

"Sorry, sorry." Bella undid her jeans as quickly as possible. She had no idea how much time had elapsed since her minute had passed, but something told her Wyatt did. She knew from past experience that he had an internal clock that worked better than the atomic clock.

She shed her jeans and panties as quickly as possible.

When she was naked she ran her fingers through her hair and waited for more instructions. They didn't come. Instead, Wyatt messed with the rope, and from where she stood it seemed as if he were making rope zip ties.

She waited.

And waited.

And waited.

Finally, Bella put her hands on her hips and said, "Well?"

"What did I say earlier?" Wyatt asked.

Bella thought about it for a moment, and then said, "I guess I wasn't listening."

"That's disappointing."

"You had me thinking about sex," she said. "I might have been slower than you wanted, but I was still thinking about getting screwed." And then it dawned on her. "The longer I take, the longer I wait."

"You were listening," Wyatt said with a chuckle. He finally stared toward her, and when he crossed behind her she turned to see what he was doing. "Did I give you permission for that? Turn back around. It's been far too long since you've followed orders. We need to work on that."

"You didn't give me an order not to move," she said. "I can't read your mind."

"How about reading my rope? Turn back around."

Bella turned her back to him, and when he next told her to clasp her hands behind her back she didn't hesitate. Wyatt pulled her hands apart, then slipped the loops around her wrists. He pulled them tight and it forced her shoulders back and her breasts seemed to lift on their own.

Wyatt stepped in front of her. He lowered his head and took one of her nipples in his mouth. Bella hissed softly as he sucked. When his mouth moved to her other nipple she arched her back as much as she could to try and push herself into his mouth.

"Hold still," he said. He lightly tapped her thigh. "If you'd been a good girl that would have been a swat, which I know you love."

"I have missed it," she admitted.

Wyatt ran his hand down her stomach, and when he reached her pussy, Bella groaned. His fingers pushed her lips apart and he found her clit. Her knees locked as he pinched and stroked her. She tried to stay still, even though he hadn't ordered her not to move.

He kept the pressure on her clit, and twice she thought she would come. But Wyatt seemed to know it, too, and he stopped moving his fingers, which made her cry out in frustration. After the second time he stood and walked to the storage shed. When he came back he had a lawn chair in his hands. He set it up and then sat down.

"What are you doing?" Her voice sounded shrill, even to her.

"I'm sorry, is it uncomfortable to be aroused and not be able to take care of it?"

For a punishment, it was, to her, over the top. Sure she'd left him in the same condition before dinner, but at least he could touch himself, even if it was just when he went to pee.

"This is so unfair," she said.

"You should have thought about it earlier," he said.

"Thought you would be vindictive?"

"This is punishment," he said. "It's not always about spankings and standing in the corner. But if you think I'm mistreating you, climb on your horse and head back to the ranch."

"Naked? With my hands tied behind my back?"

"There's a challenge to everything," Wyatt said. "If you don't want to try that, you can stand there until I'm ready to make you come. It's your choice."

She really had no choice. She didn't care about riding

naked, but she did want to come now. That meant she would be standing here until Wyatt decided to put her out of her misery.

It could be a long night.

Chapter 12

Bella didn't have an internal clock, which meant she felt as if she'd been standing in the same spot, with her clit pulsing and her nipples tingling for days. Wyatt sat in his chair, with his head tipped back to look at the stars as they appeared. At one point he got up and built a fire in the pit that wasn't far from where she stood.

After the blaze was going he walked over to her, and she hoped he was going to release her, both from her bonds, and by giving her an orgasm. When he knelt in front of her she thought he was going to do just that. He spread her pussy lips and teased her clit with his tongue. She wanted so much to touch him, to push on his head so his tongue could touch her deeper. She bucked her hips and almost lost her balance as she moved.

Wyatt grasped her hips and said, "Easy, babe, easy."

"Wyatt, I'm going crazy."

"I know," he said softly. "Tell your Master what you want."

"I want you inside me." She had three places for him to choose, and she wasn't going to make the choice for him.

"My sweet Bella wants to fuck," he said. "Do you think

I've punished you enough for sending me into dinner with a boner?"

"Fuck yes!" she screamed.

"I'm not so sure," he said. "It's only been an hour. Seems to me you should be able to wait longer." He stood and wiped his hand over his mouth. "The only problem is I want to fuck, too. So I have to make a decision. Do I satisfy my urges, and give you something you want, too? Seems to me that's not right, but at least I'll be coming."

Wyatt walked back to the chair where he'd been sitting. He bent and when he came back over to her he had more hemp rope in his hand.

Bella prayed for a whipping, and when he walked behind her she thought she might just get her wish. But then he wrapped the rope through the loops on her wrists, and then around her waist. When he'd made two loops he stepped in front of her and pulled on what was now a lead.

"Follow me," he said. They walked to where he'd unsaddled and tied up the horses. The saddles had been put on sawhorses, and he stopped in front of his. It was something she'd bought for him for Christmas years ago, hand tooled with his name written across the back jockey.

"Bend over and make yourself comfortable," he said.

His voice was like silk, and Bella bent over the saddle, her stomach cradled in the leather. Wyatt caressed her buttocks, and Bella thought he might give it to her in the ass. As she had earlier that night she waited, and waited. Wyatt continued to rub his hand across her butt, and when he finally grabbed her hips she wanted to scream at him to hurry up and fuck her.

"Speak to your Master," Wyatt said.

"Fuck me, please," she said, her voice low.

"Sounds to me like you don't give a damn," Wyatt said. "Try again."

"Fuck me, please! Fuck me."

"Wow, better, but not perfect," Wyatt said. "You're definitely out of practice."

"Whose fault is that?" she muttered.

In answer, Wyatt slapped her ass. "Are you blaming me?"

She wanted to say if he'd treated her better they would have stayed together. Instead she kept her mouth closed. If she said anything like that, she would be being bratty, and that might keep her from getting screwed right now.

"I'm sorry, Master Wyatt," she said. "I really want you to fuck me. I want to feel your dick inside me, sliding in and out, giving us both pleasure."

"Much better," he said. "As a woman who works with words, that was well done. Keep it up."

"Please give me your dick, Master." Bella wiggled her hips once again. That movement had always been one of Wyatt's favorites, but right now he didn't respond, except to caress her hips, right before he drove into her.

"Fuck yes!" Bella called out, then she giggled. Those words weren't really ones to show her language skills, but they fit for the moment.

Wyatt didn't urge her to find other words, though. He grasped her hips and thrust in and out of her. The sawhorse wobbled under her, and she worried it might collapse between the weight of the saddle, herself, and the movement of Wyatt fucking her like there was no tomorrow.

Wyatt grasped the rope around her waist and it bit into her stomach. The sawhorse was moving so fast she thought Wyatt was maybe trying to stabilize her as he rode her. A few seconds later he released his hold and slowed his movements.

He pulled his cock from her and stepped away.

"Stand up," he demanded.

Her body shook as she tried to regain control over her balance. Wyatt pulled her back into his body, his arms coming around so he could cup her breasts with his hands.

"I want to take you every way possible," he said. "Claim you as my own."

"As you wish," she answered. Her hands were very near his cock, and she tried, with no success, to touch him. He was driving her insane, taking her right to the edge and not allowing her to come. Her body quaked against him as one of his hands dropped from her breast to between her legs.

He teased her pussy lips, but didn't move his fingers inside to find her clit.

"You are driving me nuts," she said when his hands dropped away from her. "Please, Wyatt, please. I can't take anymore. I need you back inside me. Please."

She drew the last word out. He released her and it took him seconds to undo the rope around her waist and the ties around her hands.

"Arms in front," he demanded. When she'd done as he asked he tied her wrists together once again, then led her to the space where he'd laid out the sleeping bags. He lay down in the middle of them and pulled her down on top of him. She toppled and tried to steady herself after he ordered her to straddle him.

She remembered that Wyatt always loved for her to be on top once things really got going. He put his hands on her hips, which helped her to gain control of herself. Then he lifted her up and she came down on his dick, taking him deep inside her.

Wyatt bucked his hips and she started to ride him, pleasure spreading through her like wildfire. It didn't take her long to finally come, the world seeming to explode around her. Her muscles tightened around his prick, and she felt as if they were one, melded together in perfect harmony.

Wyatt bucked again, but this time he used his strength and they switched places. Bella wrapped her legs around him as he fucked her. She stared up at him, the stars twinkling above him. He rode her hard and fast, and when his body seized she knew he'd come as hard as she had. He leaned down and kissed her, pressing his lips down on hers as if he wanted to swallow her whole.

She swore she heard him mumble, "I love you," when the kiss broke, but the words were low and almost unintelligible. His body grew heavy on top of her and when he rolled to the side he undid her wrists, then got up. He left, and came back a few moments later with a wet cloth, which he used to clean between her legs, and then he ran it up and down his dick.

He tossed it aside, and then lay down next to her, gathering her in his arms. Bella snuggled against him. It was moments like this she'd missed the most, cuddling under the dark sky after she'd had him deep inside her. She prayed this wouldn't be the last time. She wanted to do this over, and over, and over again.

Bella woke to the wonderful feeling of being spooned against Wyatt's chest. He held her close, his breathing even as if he were sleeping, but his hands were moving up and down her back so she knew he was awake.

"Finally," he said. "I was beginning to think you were going to sleep until noon. I have to go feed horses and do a few other chores. You want to go with me, or do you want to stay here?"

"I have work to do, too," she said. "But I have employees who will be working, so I don't have to rush. This is the first time I've woken up outside in ages, and I'm loving it."

"Then stay here and wait for me." He kissed the back of her head and she smiled. It was so beautiful being outdoors, feeling the sunshine on a beautiful summer Texas morning. She felt Wyatt's loss when he stood. He went to use the facilities, and when he was back he'd already put on his pants. He threw on the rest of his clothes and saddled his horse.

Bella sat up and held the sheet they'd slept under up to her breasts. Watching her cowboy get ready to go work his ranch made her heart race. She wanted to tell him she loved him, she'd missed him, and last night was one of the best of her life. She hoped he felt the same.

But fear held her back. She didn't want to invest her emotions in Wyatt and end up by herself again. As much as she wanted to be with him, she was still concerned about being thrown over.

After Wyatt had saddled his horse she said, "Bring me back some coffee, and a pastry or two."

He mounted up and tipped his hat in her direction, which she took to mean yes.

As he rode off she thought about what was happening. She certainly hadn't thought she'd be back here, someplace she loved to be—The Rescue Ranch, even if she wasn't at the lake where she really wanted to be. And not just here, but with Wyatt, too. It was just so weird. She glanced at her phone. It was just after eight, which meant it was late. She called Lily, and when her office manager didn't answer, Bella left a message that she would be late, and would probably not be at the office until around ten.

There was one thing she was going to do in this almost-perfect morning, and that was take a ride to the lake. She got up, drained a bottle of water, then ate an energy bar from one of the saddlebags. A quick tour of the storage shed produced a towel. Perfect for a morning swim.

Bella saddled Austin's horse. She couldn't help but think how perfect every morning would be if she woke up in Wyatt's arms, had her own horse nearby so she could go for an early morning ride, and swim.

She mounted and started toward the lake. The only thing

that would make this glorious day better would be if Wyatt was by her side. She might not be ready to tell him she loved him, but that didn't mean she wanted to shy away from his company completely. Last night had been glorious. She wanted more times like that, and she wanted time with her Daddy, too.

Bella needed to figure out the exact words to let Wyatt know that. She was afraid she would start to speak, then stutter and stumble over her words. Or maybe she should just do something deserving of punishment and let Wyatt take over from there. That would probably be best. He was good at taking charge.

As she neared the lake she stopped and cocked her head. Was it her imagination, or did she hear the laughter of children? Only one of the brothers, Holt and his wife Aurora, had a child, but this was the laughter of older children, she would say at least age five and up.

She was near the road that led from the main ranch house to the lake. There was no one around. She kicked the horse into gear and the closer she got to the lake the louder the laughter became. At the top of a hill she stopped and looked down.

There was an all-terrain vehicle parked at the lake. Sitting at the picnic table was a woman that Bella guessed to be in her thirties. There were three children playing in the lake, splashing water at each other, and passing around a beach ball.

Bella tried to process what she was seeing. This was private property, so someone couldn't just drive down here and use the lake as a play place. She had to be a guest of one of the brothers. Since three of them were now married, and three were single, that cut the odds somewhat.

To her, you'd have to know someone pretty well to allow her to come to your land and let her kids play in the lake. And there was only one way to find out who this person was, and that was to go and ask her.

Bella rode up to where the woman sat, her gaze trained on the children as they played.

"Good morning," Bella said at the same time one of the children said, "Look Mommy, horsey!"

The woman jumped up from her seat and said, "Oh my, did I miss an announcement you would be here? I'm so sorry. Holt usually calls and lets me know when a new client will be here. I'm Becky."

"Bella." Bella dismounted, since all three of the kids were out of the water and running toward the horse.

"Careful," their mother ordered. "Don't touch unless Miss Bella says it's okay."

"This is Lawrence, and he's Austin's horse," Bella said. "This is only the second time I've ridden him, but I do think you can pet his nose one at a time. Gently."

Lawrence lowered his head as each of the children gently patted him. When they were done they ran back to the lake.

When they were gone, Becky said, "I'm so sorry I didn't get the message from Holt that you were coming. Which house are you staying at?"

Bella shook her head in confusion. "House? I'm not here to stay in a house. I'm a friend of Wyatt's and I'm just out for a ride."

"Oh thank God," Becky said. "I was afraid I was falling down on the job."

Job? What was she talking about? "Looks like the kids are having fun."

"They love the lake," Becky said.

Bella's phone, which had been tucked into her saddlebag in case Lily called her back, rang. She excused herself and walked to Lawrence's side. Instead of Lily's name on the display she saw Wyatt's.

"Where are you?" he barked out when she'd answered the phone.

"At the lake, talking to Becky," she said innocently.

"I told you to stay here," he said.

"Did you?" She laughed softly. "But then I never would have met Becky."

"Get back here. Now."

"Becky and I are talking about houses," Bella said.

"Now," Wyatt repeated.

"I miss you too, darling." She disconnected the call and waved at the kids, who were not paying attention. Becky had been watching them, not her.

"I have to go," she said. "It was wonderful to meet you."

"Come back soon," Becky called out as Bella mounted her horse. Something told her she would not be back any time soon if Wyatt had anything to do with it.

Chapter 13

Normally, when Wyatt saw Bella riding toward him he would be thrilled. Nothing like the sight of her in the saddle made him happier. But right now he was angry with her for disobeying him, and with himself for not thinking she would go off on her own. He knew her better than that. Last night she had been excited about going to the lake. When his brothers found out she'd visited on her own they would not be happy with him for giving her the opportunity.

She'd have questions, and he'd have to tell her the truth, and then he'd have to punish her for going off on her own.

Bella rode up next to him and, from the back of the horse, she said, "Who is Becky and why was she asking me about a house?"

"Get down off that horse," he ordered.

"Answer my question," she said. "Do you have something going on with that woman?"

"I said, get down," he replied, his voice steely.

She glared down at him, a look he'd seen so many times in their relationship. Bella was nothing if not headstrong.

"Why did you lie to me?" she asked.

"When did I lie?" He grabbed Lawrence's reins and repeated, "Get down."

At first he thought she was going to say no, but then she dismounted and stood right next to him. She pointed her finger in his face. "You did. Last night, you didn't tell me about Becky."

"I didn't lie to you," he said.

"Not telling me why we couldn't go to the lake is just like lying," she said. "You have something going on with this woman?"

Wyatt snorted out a laugh. "She's engaged to a Texas Ranger, so no, I don't."

"Then who the fuck is she?"

"Watch your mouth."

"Fuck you!" She jabbed her finger into his chest. "I should have known you wouldn't be honest with me. You never are."

"I'm sorry you seem to think not telling you something is lying." He shrugged and took a step back from the finger that was still poking into him. "Becky and the houses is not my secret to tell without permission from my family."

"What the fuck does that mean?"

"Stop cussing!" This time he poked his finger into her chest.

"Fuck you!"

"If I had a bar of soap you'd be tasting it right now."

"I want you to tell me the fucking truth!"

"No, what you want is to know everything, about everyone," he said. "I know it's your job to spread news, but Becky is not news. She is just part of life in Bookman Springs."

"Do you fucking let everyone in Bookman swim in your lake?"

"Watch your fucking mouth!"

Bella pushed on his shoulders with such force that he almost lost his balance.

"You're an ass!"

"And you expect too much," he said. He turned and started toward the storage shed.

"Where are you going? Running from the issue like always?" she yelled as he walked off.

"I'm going to look for a bar of soap," he said. "Something to clean up that mouth of yours."

He entered the storage shed, which had anything a person would need for camping, which included a box of personal hygiene supplies. There was a bottle of liquid soap and a bar of soap. He grabbed the bar and headed out the door, only to see Bella riding off on Lawrence.

"Get back here," he yelled after her.

She didn't even look in his direction, she just kept going. He tried to tell himself she wasn't running from him in what would be their first Daddy/little scene since they'd reconnected. Maybe something had happened and she needed to go. He hoped that was the case. Because if not she would be doing more than taking a bite out of soap.

Bella had one hand on the reins, and one on her phone. Lily sounded frazzled and her words made Bella shiver.

"I've already called Hawk," Lily said. "I have no idea why the alarm didn't go off, but every window is broken."

Frank would blame this on her, Bella was sure of that. Insurance would cover it, but he would still say if she'd let go of the theft issue whoever had busted every window in the newspaper office wouldn't have done it. As she thought about it, the idea of her SUV sitting behind the office, took front and center.

"What about my vehicle?" she asked.

"I didn't look," Lily said. "I figured it was with you. Kirk, go to the alley and check on Bella's truck."

"Is anything missing?" Bella asked.

"Every computer in the newsroom," Lily said. "Just the CPUs, not the monitors."

"Someone wanted to keep tomorrow's newspaper from coming out," Bella said. "Listen, call Hawk back and tell him I need a ride from the ranch."

"You little imp," Lily said. "Did you get laid?"

"That's not important right now," Bella said. Although running out on Wyatt when he meant to punish her for cussing up a storm like she had wasn't a good thing. He would be really pissed when he saw she was gone. She should have stayed there and told him what had happened. But she was already frazzled by meeting Becky, and Wyatt refusing to tell her what the woman really meant and then to have Lily call and say, in a panicked voice, "Someone broke into the office last night. It's a mess."

Bella had taken off as fast as she could get Lawrence to run. She knew she should call her mother, and her brothers, but the newspaper was her responsibility, and frankly she didn't want to talk to Frank, or her mother.

Lily had disconnected to call Hawk. Bella stopped Lawrence and called Sam. The first question he asked when she told him what had happened validated her choice.

"Are you okay?"

"Fine," she said. "I wasn't at home last night. I'm about to head to the office."

"I'll meet you there," Sam said.

The phone went dead, and seconds later it rang again. It was Wyatt.

"I'm sorry," she said, but before she could say more he

said, "Holt called and told me what happened. Don't leave the ranch without me. I'm going with you."

It was on the tip of her tongue to tell him she didn't need him, but despite the fact she was pissed at him, having him near her would be comforting.

She found Austin waiting by the stables. After she dismounted she offered to unsaddle Lawrence, but Austin told her to go to the house. Austin told her Hawk had called and said he was already at the newspaper with several deputies, and she could ride to the office with Wyatt.

"There's food and coffee inside the house," Austin said. "In fact, Jessica is packing boxes of pastries to take down, and a few thermoses of coffee. Holt's going to take them down."

Bella turned at the sound of hoof beats. Wyatt was there in seconds. He jumped down from his horse and handed Austin the reins.

"Keep me informed about what's happening," Austin called after them as they headed toward the house. Bella made a stop in the bathroom where she brushed her teeth with a brush Wyatt gave to her. She'd watched as he'd retrieved it from a closet, and she wondered what else he had in there, maybe items he kept for ladies who stayed the night with no provisions.

It made her wonder once again about Becky, and other women who might be roaming around the ranch. But she had other things she needed to be thinking about right now. Lily had not called her back with any more information.

When she came out of the bathroom Wyatt waited at the front door. He'd changed his shirt, and he jingled his keys from his fingers.

"Let's go," he said.

It didn't take long to get to the square, and they rode in silence. When Wyatt parked in front of the newspaper office, Bella was surprised to see a number of people standing around, watching. There were at least twenty people, standing across the street, with more sitting in their cars.

"That's what happens when you live in a town that has no crime," Wyatt said. "When something happens, everyone in town shows up to watch."

"True," Bella said softly, as she got out of the truck. Hawk walked up to her and offered his hand. She shook it, and then turned to the sheriff, who was right behind Hawk.

"You piss someone off with an article?" the sheriff, Landon Parker, asked.

"It's a way of life, Landon," Bella said. "People don't want their arrests reported, so they get pissed. But this isn't about an arrest."

"Yeah, Hawk filled me in about the threat, and the demand for the necklace." The sheriff pulled out his phone. "And there is this."

Bella stared at the photo on Landon's phone. It was of her front door, which was intact, with 'Where is my necklace', spray painted on it.

"Do you have the necklace?' Landon asked.

"I have no idea what they are talking about," Bella said. "We're trying to get to the bottom of a mystery, and it has ticked someone off."

"I think that word is too light to use," Hawk said. "Let's go inside. But brace yourself."

The lawmen ushered Bella inside, with Wyatt right behind her. She stopped dead in her tracks and tears filled her eyes. It was as if someone had taken an ax to the entire newsroom. Framed historical copies of the newspaper had been torn from the walls. All the desks had been wiped clean of every scrap of paper, and each desk had been covered with paint. Chairs had been overturned, and the paint had also been splashed on the hardwood floors.

"This is your fault." Frank's voice filled the room. "If you had done like I said, this wouldn't have happened."

Sam yelled at Frank, "Shut the fuck up."

Wyatt stepped up next to her and put his arm around her shoulders.

"Point the finger at yourself," Wyatt said.

"Excuse me?" Frank asked.

"What he means is if you and your friends hadn't stolen the items in the first place, none of this would have happened," Bella said. She didn't care that she was pointing the finger at her own brother. She knew he was guilty, and she didn't care who she told.

"I can't believe you just accused me of being a thief," Frank said.

"You and your friends," Wyatt said.

"You keep out of this." Frank pointed his finger at Wyatt.

"I've been accused of your misdeed for years," Wyatt yelled. "I have every right to be in this discussion. Plus, I don't like you treating Bella like dirt."

"You would know about that," Frank said. "You've never treated her right."

"Keep your nose out of my relationship," Bella said. "Wyatt's right. He was blamed for years for what you did. Deny it all you want, but the only reason Dad would have protected thieves is if one of them was his own son."

She could see by the look on Frank's face that he was guilty. She looked at Sam, who was staring at their brother, his expression one of surprise.

"She's telling the truth, isn't she?" Sam said. "I can tell by your expression. Who did it with you? Who is doing this now? Who is threatening our sister?"

"I have no idea what you are talking about," Frank said.

"You mother fucker!" Sam yelled and charged at Frank,

and Bella dove into the fray, as she'd always done with her brothers.

Before she could get a good punch in, though, Wyatt grabbed her around the waist. "Don't baby," he whispered in her ear.

Hawk and Landon were pulling the brothers apart. When they were standing, Bella was happy to see Frank had a bloody nose, and Sam only had a busted lip.

"Frank, if what Bella is saying is true, then you should know you can't be charged," Landon said. "The statute of limitations is long past. But if you can help us figure out who did this, then people will take notice."

"In other words they'll forget you stole things from the museum," Wyatt said.

"You're not helping," Hawk said.

Frank shook his head. "I swear, I don't know who did this."

Bella noticed he didn't deny the museum theft again, which seemed to her to be a step in the right direction.

"Does Mom know?" Sam asked. He bent down to pick up his hat, which he'd lost in the fight. "Of course she does. You were always her favorite. You ass."

"It was just a prank," Frank said. "The stuff was in the alley, and we were back there to egg Abby's car because the bitch had screamed at us earlier in the day for laughing at her as she kicked someone out of the museum."

"Frank, who's we?" Hawk asked. "And what do you mean it was in the alley?"

"They were in boxes, in the alley," Frank said. "We just took it and didn't think about it."

"Frank, who's we?" It was Landon who asked this time.

Frank shook his head. "I'm not ratting them out."

"Even if it means figuring out who is threatening Bella?" Sam asked.

"Neither of them would have done this," Frank said. "This has to be because of something Bella did."

"You are full of crap!" Bella wanted to slap him. But Wyatt stepped in front of her and stroked her shoulders.

"Babe, you can't get him to change his mind. You know this isn't because of you, but because of something he did."

"Get your hands off my sister," Frank said. "You've hurt her too much in her life. She doesn't need you."

"He's the only one I need," Bella said. "Let's not forget I have a brother who has lied to me for fourteen years. Not just to me, but to our entire town."

"What about the necklace?" Sam asked. "Was there a necklace in the stash you took?"

A wall went up on Frank's face, and Bella knew there was one, and he knew where it was right now. There was only one place that made sense.

"Mom has it," Bella said. "That's why she was so mad at Dad for bringing Reed into it, and mad at me for keeping it going. She'll never give it up."

"I'll talk to her," Landon said.

"She won't listen to you," Sam said. "Let me talk to her."

Bella didn't argue with that. She knew Frank wouldn't step up, and her mother was more likely to listen to one of her brothers than she was to Bella.

"They took every computer?" Bella asked.

"Lily says every one of them," Landon said. "The surprising thing to me is they didn't go into your apartment."

"It's a steel door," Wyatt said.

"Why wasn't the alarm on?" Frank asked, his tone placing the blame on her.

"That would be my fault," Lily said from behind them. "I thought Jack was still here. I didn't set it when I left because of that."

"Bella should have been here instead of out screwing

around," Frank said. "It's her responsibility." He glared at Wyatt, and Bella stepped in front of Wyatt.

"It amazes me that you refuse to take responsibility for being a thief, but you're quick to throw out blame." She wanted to slap her brother.

"I told you it was a prank," Frank said.

"A prank where you took things that didn't belong to you," Bella said.

"My question is what was it doing in the alley?" Wyatt asked.

"Good question," Hawk said. "I guess we need to talk to Abby."

"She'll talk to me," Landon said. "She and my mom are friends."

"Can we start cleaning up this mess?" Bella asked Landon.

"Yes, we have photos of it all," Landon said. "What about your paper for tomorrow?"

"It's all done electronically now," Bella said. "We store stories and photos in the cloud, so we have everything. We just have to find a computer to put it together."

"Boss, remember I have the software loaded on my computer at home from when I worked in production," Lilly said. "I'll bring my computer down and we'll do it on there. I just want to say, though, that I did say you needed more than a laptop at home."

Bella couldn't help but laugh. "You're right, of course. I will do that when we replace these. While Lily goes after her computer, we'll start cleaning.'

The group broke apart, and about half an hour later, Bella looked up to see the remaining Coleman brothers and their wives.

Bella glanced over to where Wyatt stood, a trash bag in his hand. "I asked them to help," he said. "I hope that's okay with you."

"It's perfect," Bella said. "And so are you. Thank you so much."

"Anything for you," Wyatt said, and her heart swelled.

After this she would feel better with him by her side tonight. She needed to lean on him, to feel his strength.

Tonight she would tell him she still loved him, and she needed him. She prayed it would end well.

Chapter 14

Bella's Musings
By Bella Beaumont
© *The Bookman Gazette*

This is the third time I have written this week's column. Fine tuning my words is sometimes hard to do, and that's what the second rewrite was about. And then yesterday happened. For those of you who haven't heard it through the Bookman grapevine, someone broke into the Gazette office Monday night. They vandalized the offices and stole every computer.

Their motivation? To keep information about the museum theft from fourteen years ago from getting out. We reported when the items were recovered, but what many people don't know is this weekend I received a letter threatening both myself and Wyatt Coleman about the return of a necklace, the theft of which was never reported.

We are sure the same burglars were involved in the

museum. Sheriff Landon Parker wanted me to remind everyone that the statute of limitations on the museum theft makes it that whoever did it can't be charged.

But they can be charged with what happened at the newspaper office. Because of the damage, and the amount of computers taken, the charges would be a felony. If you have overheard someone bragging about what they have done, please let me know, or report the information to Sheriff Parker, or Constable Hawk Coleman.

Breaking into a business, no matter what leads you to do it, shouldn't be tolerated in Bookman Springs. I don't care if it's my business, or any other business in town. So keep your ears open, and let me know what you hear.

They didn't make it up to her apartment until after midnight, which was disappointing to Bella because she had things she wanted to say, things she wanted to do. But they got the paper rebuilt and the files uploaded to Lubbock where it was printed. Whoever had wanted to stop production had failed.

The Colemans had stayed until the last minute, until every scrap of paper had been picked up, and every spray of paint had been removed from the walls. Austin had gone home in the afternoon to prepare a meal for her staff, and for that she'd been extremely grateful. It had been a delicious meal of fried chicken and potato salad. She'd made a mental note to send them all a thank you note, or maybe think of some other way to express her gratitude.

When they were all gone, she and Wyatt had gone up to her apartment, where even the spray paint had been cleaned up. Wyatt sat down on the couch the moment they were inside.

"Don't get too comfortable there," Bella said. She went to the refrigerator and made a plate of cheese and crackers. It was her nightly snack, and she'd missed it last night. But it had been replaced with terrific sex under the stars, so it was all good.

"Are you going to try and kick me out?" Wyatt said.

"After what you did for me today? Um, no," she said.

"I figured you were still pissed about the Becky thing," he said. "Although you left the camping site when I told you not to."

Becky… she'd forgotten about Becky. "So tell me about Becky," she said.

Wyatt took a deep breath, and it seemed to her as if he were about to let go of a state secret. "Becky is our den mother."

"Excuse me?"

"We don't just rescue horses at the ranch," Wyatt said. "We have cabins where ladies who are running from abusive relationships can hide."

"What?" She sat down next to him on the couch and put the cheese plate on his thigh. "How do you find clients? Do you advertise things like that?"

"We are state run," Wyatt said. "Ladies who are looking for a place to stay for a while can go through a state agency. We have six cabins we can fill, and Becky is our house mother."

Bella couldn't believe what she was hearing. "Who decided on this? Holt? Hawk?"

"Actually my parents started it years ago," he said. "We took over when they retired."

"What? You've been doing this all these years?" Bella asked.

"The location is supposed to be kept secret, to protect the clients."

"I see." Bella took a bite of cheese on a cracker. "Thus the huge fence," she said after she swallowed."

She listened as Wyatt told her about a thief, who had been looking for information on the museum theft who had jumped the fence to break into the house. "We want our ladies to be safe," he said.

"Hearing that makes me love you even more than I have before," Bella said.

"Even more?" Wyatt asked. "I thought your love for me had died."

"My love never died," she said. "I allowed you to bruise me, true, but I should have screamed, hollered, hit you, and worked through it."

"You did scream, holler, and hit me," he said. "By the way, isn't scream and holler the same thing?"

"What, you're a writer now?" she asked. She ate another slice of cheese.

"Only trying to make you better at your job," Wyatt said with a chuckle.

"This coming from a cowboy," she said with a soft laugh.

"This coming from your Daddy, who wants you to be the best at everything," he said. "And it's been a very stressful day for you, from start to finish. I want you to go to sleep now, to relax and know we're going to get to the bottom of things."

"Speaking of which, I think I know a way to figure out who is doing the threats, identify Frank's accomplice," she said. "I remember his friends from back then. If it was a prank—"

Wyatt put his hand over her mouth. "Like I said, a stressful day. You need sleep. We'll discuss this in the morning. Right now, my Baby Bella needs to close her eyes and let the sandman come."

"We need to figure this out," she said, her words ending on a yawn.

"You need to sleep," he said. "Today has not been a good day for you." He stood and offered her his hand. "Let's go to bed. No hanky panky tonight. Daddy orders you to sleep."

He was surprised when she put her hand in his and stood. "I need to put up the leftover cheese," she said. He could hear the disappointment in her voice.

"Here's what we do," Wyatt said. "We'll take it to bed, and then watch some cartoons until you fall asleep."

"Sounds like fun," she said. "I have a bottle of wine in the fridge."

"We'll have sodas," Wyatt said. "Daddy's little girl does not drink wine."

"What about rum?" she asked. "I could use a drink tonight."

"You could use some cuddles," he said. "Fix us two sodas and come to bed."

"Yes, Daddy," she said.

Wyatt watched as she walked to the kitchen. He would love to take her tonight, but he knew she needed sleep. Between the discovery of her brother as the museum thief, and the break-in at the newspaper office, she'd had a very trying day. He wanted her to laugh, to forget everything that happened, to fall asleep in his arms.

Truthfully, he wanted her to sleep in his arms for the rest of their lives. She'd told him she loved him. That was a step forward. But it didn't mean she wouldn't step away again if he screwed things up.

He had to treat her like a queen, and let her know they were meant to be together… forever.

Bella giggled as the roadrunner pulled up the asphalt and turned it so the coyote ran off a cliff. These were her favorite cartoons. She'd watched them since she was a kid, and she loved every second of them. Right now, though, she wished she was the roadrunner and her brother Frank was dropping off the cliff.

"I wonder if Landon talked to Mom," she whispered.

"Hey, what did I tell you about forgetting everything and just enjoying yourself? It's almost three o'clock in the morning, and I'm letting you stay up past your bedtime. You need to take advantage of it and relax. Either that or Daddy is shutting off the TV and we're going to sleep."

Bella hated that idea. She was much calmer now than she had been an hour ago. The stress from the day had melted away as she'd snuggled against Wyatt and they'd laughed together.

Why Frank had come back into her mind, she wasn't sure. But she knew he would be there tomorrow, and at some point she would have to face her mother.

"Can we stay here all day tomorrow, Daddy?" she asked. "I don't want to face the world."

"We'll face it together," he said. "I already talked to Kyle and asked him to feed horses in the morning and he agreed, but I'll owe him one, or maybe two. But being with my Baby Bella will be worth it."

She snuggled against his chest. "Thank you, Daddy."

"Anything for you, baby girl."

This was like her fantasy come true. The only problem was fantasies were not real life. Real life was finding the man you love in the arms of two other women. She wanted this to last, but if she did would he screw her over again? Could she trust him?

"You've stiffened up," Wyatt said. "Are you upset because the coyote took a dive? Or are you thinking about what happened today?"

It was best to be truthful, Bella thought. "I'm thinking of you. I love you, and this is so wonderful. But I'm scared."

To his credit, he didn't ask why she was scared. He knew it was because of his wandering eye—or more to the point his wandering dick.

"Bella, I would love to assure you I'll never do it again." He wrapped his arms around her and she waited for his but. "Given what I did to you before there's no reason why you should believe me. But I promise you, my dick only wants to be inside you, my arms only want to be around you, and my heart wants to love only you."

Tears filled her eyes as he spoke. He'd never said anything like that to her before.

"Can we make it work?" she managed to say.

"I do believe we can," Wyatt said. "Your family will not be happy about it."

"True," she said. "But I believe my father will be smiling down at us. No matter what Mom said, he always liked you."

"That really makes me feel good," Wyatt said. "You know not everybody in town thinks I'm a good person. And they will think you're weak for taking me back after I cheated on you."

"Fuck them," Bella said. "It's none of their business. Unless we get married, and then divorced, then it gets listed in the public records section. Or if one of us gets arrested. I don't plan on doing something to get arrested, do you?"

"Not at this moment," Wyatt said. "But you know I do tend to piss people off."

He kissed the top of her head. "So are you asking me to marry you?" he asked.

"I don't believe I said the words," she replied.

"You're talking about marriage and divorce." He kissed the top of her head again. "If you're not asking me, I'll ask you. Bella, will you marry me? Will you be my wife, and my little?"

"Are you going to put the little part into our vows?" she asked. "It would freak a lot of our guests out."

"That will be for us when we're alone," he said. "Separate vows."

"That works for me," Bella said. "Does this mean we're engaged? After we've only been together for what, four days?"

"To me that means we were always meant to be together," Wyatt said. "We love each other. We always have. I just put a dent in it and now we're buffing it out."

"Were we waiting for an insurance claim?"

"No, just for me to claim fault," he said. "I'm not very good at that."

"I hope we don't have to test that theory out in our marriage," she said.

"I plan on behaving and taking care of you," Wyatt said. "I'll even put it in writing. In fact, you can write it for me. You're good at that."

"I'll take your word for it," Bella said. "I trust you again."

"And I love you," Wyatt said. "And I don't want to do anything to mess up the fact you love me again."

Bella kissed his shoulder and whispered, "Don't worry, you won't."

Chapter 15

"Don't walk out that door without breakfast," Wyatt called out from the kitchen.

Bella stopped in her tracks, one hand on her portable coffee cup, the other on the doorknob. She held up her coffee mug. "I have breakfast, thank you very much."

"Boy it's a good thing you're going to be living with your Daddy," Wyatt said. "Breakfast is the most important meal of the day. I've made some sausage and toast, so get your butt back in here and eat."

"I don't eat breakfast," she said. "I would have thought you'd remember that."

"As your Daddy, I'm telling you to come and eat," Wyatt said.

"You never forced me to eat before," she complained.

"Daddy's a little stricter now," Wyatt replied. "Come and eat, or go and stand in the corner."

"You have got to be kidding me," Bella said.

"Are you sassing me?"

"You bet your ass I am," she said. "Being force-fed fucking sucks."

"You know, I was looking for soap when you ran off the other day." Wyatt waved a piece of toast in her direction. "I don't like you using fuck all the time."

"I don't!" Bella shrugged. "Plus, you say it, too. If you make me bite soap, I'm going to do the same to you."

"Get over here and eat," Wyatt said.

"If you're going to be so controlling over my food intake, I might reconsider the contract idea," she said. "You can't tell me when and what to eat."

"I just want you to start the day off right," he said.

"You're being controlling," she said. "Even my real father didn't make such a fuss over me eating."

"I can't believe he never said you had to sit at the table until your plate was clean."

She didn't have an answer for that, because it had happened more than once in her childhood.

Finally she said, "That was Mom's line. Dad would usually say, 'Bitsy, let her eat what she wants'."

"I want us to share meals," he said. "I want us to be a family, even if it's just the two of us."

"What about when there's a little Wyatt?" she asked softly.

"First off, he'll have his own name, and second off, there will be more than toast and sausage for breakfast." His smile brightened his face. "I'll have Austin teach me how to make pancakes."

Bella couldn't help but laugh. "And I'll be your taste-tester." She sat down at the table and slathered a piece of toast with raspberry jam, then did the same to a second. She made herself a sausage sandwich and took a bite. It was really tasty, but that didn't mean she planned on having breakfast every morning, even if there were pancakes on the menu.

"I have to buy computers today, and set up the office. But tonight we need to sit down and figure out who my brother's thieving partner was, because he will never tell us."

"How should we do that?" Wyatt asked.

"We need to go back in time, in our minds, and remember who my brother hung out with. It won't take us long to figure out who helped him."

"Good plan," Wyatt said. "Whoever it was is the one sending the threats, which are still real, so please be careful today."

"You, too," she said. "Despite your high fence and security system."

"I have a rifle on my saddle," he said. "Do you have a gun in your desk?"

Bella shook her head. "I never felt the need," she said. Until now, she thought to herself.

"After yesterday, I don't think anyone is going to come into the office," Wyatt said. "Hawk will be watching the place like, well, like a hawk. I have a feeling Landon will have deputies in town, too."

"Sounds good," Bella said. She had so much to do downstairs, but in her mind she was thinking about her brother's friends, and who could be the one threatening them. The two things warred for dominance in her brain, but she knew the office took the lead. They had to get things set back up for next week's paper. She had a responsibility to the town to get it done.

"I wonder if Dad knew giving back the artifacts would cause such a ruckus," she said.

"Doubtful," Wyatt said. "I'm going to the Ranch now. I'll call you later to discuss lunch."

"You going to force-feed me that, too?" she asked with a laugh.

"It'll be something Austin made," Wyatt said. "Everybody wants to eat his cooking, so I won't have to force-feed you."

"That's true," Bella said with a laugh. She tilted her head

and puckered her lips. She'd thought to give him an air kiss, but he leaned over and planted his lips on hers.

"That's a perfect way to start the morning," Bella said.

"I agree," Wyatt said, right before he kissed her again.

A little after eleven, Landon walked through her office door. Bella and Lily had spent the morning ordering new computers from an office supply store in town, which didn't have them in stock, but promised they'd be delivered in two days.

Bella always liked to give her business to locally owned shops.

She had an appointment with her insurance agent at three, who would start the claim process. She worried that they'd cleaned up before he saw the damage, but they had photos of everything.

She was making notes when Landon came in. He placed a manila envelope on her desk and sat down in a chair.

"What's this?" she asked just as Wyatt walked in.

"It's the necklace," Landon said. "I convinced your mother it would be good for her reputation if she gave it to me of her own free will."

Wyatt sat down next to Landon, and Bella stared at the envelope. She wanted to open it and see what was inside, but first she had questions that needed to be answered. Before she could say anything, Wyatt grabbed the envelope and took out the necklace.

It was made of beads, and it was beautiful.

"Why wasn't this reported as stolen?" Wyatt said.

"Well, I've talked to Abby about that," Landon said. "Seems she was selling artifacts out the back door, which is why the things were in the alley. She was waiting for her buyer."

"That fucking bitch," Wyatt said.

"Well, there's good news and bad news on that front," Landon said. "She's still doing it."

"That fucking bitch," Bella said, and they all laughed.

"She's being processed at the sheriff's department," Landon continued after the laughter died."

"She's under arrest?" Bella asked. She had two reporters, and she needed to get this information to one of them so it could be in next week's paper. "How did you figure out what she was doing?"

"Believe it or not from Frank," Landon said. "When he mentioned he'd found the things in the alley, I asked her what they were doing there. I did that yesterday. She hemmed and hawed and couldn't come up with a good excuse, so I called Mimmie Black, the head of the museum board. They were there at seven this morning, and it didn't take them long to do a quick inventory and figure out things were missing. We arrested her at ten."

"One second." Bella picked up her phone and hit Lily's extension. "Find Paul and tell him to come to my office ASAP."

Both Wyatt and Landon were staring at her when she put the phone back down. "I want him to find out when the arraignment is, so we can get pictures."

"Good," Wyatt said. "Plaster them all over the front page."

"Above the fold," Bella said. "Did Frank let out who his accomplices were?"

"Nope," Landon said. "And he's not going to. Sorry. Which means I'll have to figure it out."

"We'll do it," Wyatt said.

"No, you won't," Landon replied. "Let law enforcement handle it."

Bella shot Wyatt a look that she hoped he understood—to keep his mouth shut so Landon would think they would keep out of it. He nodded at her ever so slowly, and she knew he understood.

"Listen you two, whoever is leaving those notes is danger-ous. Let the professionals handle it."

"Investigative journalists sometimes get to the bottom of things," Bella said. "I think that makes me a professional. Plus, I'm woman enough to admit I was wrong. She did send the notes, didn't she? She vandalized the newspaper office. She wanted that necklace."

"Yes, to all points. But I still don't want you poking your nose into this anymore," Landon said. "Look at what they did to the newspaper office. I talked to Abby before I arrested her. That necklace could be sold on the black market for a hundred thousand dollars. People kill for that amount of money."

"Then you call Toby at the radio station and have him announce that you have the necklace," she said. "I'll have it put up on the website."

"That doesn't mean whoever it is won't come after you," Landon said. "Leave it alone."

He stood and picked up the envelope. "I'll let you know what I find out."

Bella saw Paul standing in the doorway. She told him to go to the courthouse to get the latest on Abby, and to make sure it was put on the website as soon as possible.

"Got it, Boss," he said. "Exciting news day."

"Very," Bella agreed.

When he was gone, Wyatt stood up. "I have a picnic in the truck. Let's enjoy some outdoor air."

"It needs to be a fast lunch," she said. "I have lots of work that needs to be done, especially with this latest museum development."

"Which you just assigned to Paul," Wyatt said. "You need the afternoon off."

"I have a business to run," Bella said. She picked up a pen, dropped it back on the desk, then picked it up again.

"Not for long."

Bella looked up to see Frank standing in the doorway. The anger that radiated from her brother filled the room.

"What are you talking about?" Bella asked.

"Mother, as the head of the corporation that runs this newspaper, wants you gone," Frank said. "She's called an emergency board meeting for tomorrow morning to have you ousted."

Bella fell back into her chair. "You're joking."

"I'm very serious," he said.

"So you'll protect your thieving friends, but grind your little sister under your boot heels," Wyatt said.

"Stay out of this Coleman, it's a family thing," Frank said.

"Since your sister and I are going to get married, I would say we're family," Wyatt answered.

Frank's loud exhale made Bella laugh.

"What's wrong, afraid I'll ruin the family reputation?" She picked up her pen and threw it at him. "Don't worry, you've already done that. Everybody in town knows you did it, but can't be charged. I'm sure it will be on the radio soon, since Abby was arrested today for selling artifacts out the back door. Somehow it will slip that Frank Beaumont and his buddies were responsible for the theft."

"Are you threatening me?"

"Isn't that what you're doing to me?" Bella stood. "Since you're ousting me, you can take over now. Meet with the insurance agent at three. And pay the bills today. And make sure the website is up to date. And make sure to answer the phones today and talk to readers about today's issue. We always get lots of calls. I'm taking the afternoon off."

"You have work to do," Frank said.

"You expect me to stay here and work when you've just

told me you're firing me? Up yours." She rounded the desk and Wyatt stood up and put his arm around her.

"By the way, Frank," Wyatt said. "The retirees at the bakery were already gossiping about you and your friends stealing from the museum all those years ago, so if you and your mother can Bella, everyone will know why. So good luck with that reputation thing. When you're a dick, everyone knows."

"Don't you dare talk to me like that," Frank said.

"I dare anything I fucking well please," Wyatt said. "You're the one throwing your sister under the bus for something you did. It's a shame, isn't it?"

Wyatt moved his hand to the small of her back and gently led her past Frank, who hadn't responded. There was a hole in her stomach now, one that would continue to grow and eat up her insides. Thank God for Wyatt, who right now was her rock.

"I need to talk to Lily," she said.

"You're really going to give up that easily?" Wyatt whispered near her ear. "That's not the Bella I've always known and loved."

"You want me to go against my whole family?" She moved toward Lily's desk. "I'm leaving for the day. Frank will meet with the insurance adjuster."

"Okay," Lily said uncertainly. Bella knew she was thinking the same thing as Wyatt… what was happening?

"I'll be back in the morning," Bella assured her.

Lily's face brightened. "Sounds good, Boss."

The moment she said that, tears filled Bella's eyes. She blinked them away, and she knew Wyatt was right. She couldn't—wouldn't—give up that easily. She would fight for her job, for the newspaper, for her integrity. If she could convince Sam and Jesse to join her, she would win. She could count on Sam, but getting a vote from Jesse might prove difficult. But she wasn't going to call him and beg. She would make her case tomorrow, and she would be strong.

"What can I do for you?" Wyatt asked once they were in the truck. She knew he'd recognized her change of mind while they were at Lily's desk.

"I need to refocus," she said. "I need my Daddy."

"He's here, but right now he's hungry. But after we eat, he's going to pump up your courage, and remind you to go after what you deserve."

Chapter 16

Bella was a little surprised when he drove out of town, until he turned off the main highway onto what was fondly called Depot Road. When the railroad came through the area, the town founders figured out an area that was best for it, and the railroad ended up going in about ten miles east, right through the middle of the small town.

A town founder had taken the depot and turned it into a house, and it had been sold several times until the 1950s, when it had been vacated and had stayed that way. In their early years together, Bella and Wyatt had used it as a spot to be alone, where they could talk, play out Daddy scenes, and noisy BDSM play.

After they'd broken up she would drive out here and sit and cry, until the day she decided she wouldn't cry over Wyatt anymore. She had no idea if Wyatt had ever come back here, but the fact he brought her here said he had memories of it, too, ones that haunted him, too.

Wyatt parked around back, as he always did when they were younger, so no one saw the truck from the main road. He got out, opened the back door and took out the picnic basket, then came around and opened her door.

"You should have brought chairs," she said. "I bet this place is filthy, and I do want to be back in time for the meeting, in clean clothes."

"What meeting?" Wyatt asked.

"With the insurance guy," she said. "I've changed my mind about Frank handling it. It's like I'm giving up, and I'm not ready to do that."

Wyatt winked at her. "That's my girl."

She poked him in the chest. "Don't ever call me girl. I'm a woman."

He opened the door and let her inside. She was surprised to see the floor had been swept. There was a card table set up with two folding chairs. Once he shut the door it was dark inside. She heard a click and turned to see him holding a flashlight. He put the basket on the table, then fished a lighter out of his pocket. The candles on the table gave off a romantic glow. Wyatt held out a chair and she sat down. Once he opened the basket he took out several sandwiches and a container that he set on the table.

"Leftovers from yesterday," he said. "Potato salad, and brisket sandwiches."

"There's a lot of memories in this building," she said.

"I bought it," Wyatt said, "about four years ago."

Bella stared at him. "I don't remember seeing the sale listed in the public records. The tax office releases information to us about sales every month."

"It was listed in the paper," he said as he unwrapped a sandwich. "But you weren't editor, or publisher, or whatever it is you are now."

"That's why I didn't hear about it," she said. "I'm going to have to work hard to keep that job. I'm sure Mom is telling my brothers to vote against me."

"You going to call and tell them otherwise?" he asked.

"No." She took a bite of her sandwich. It was delicious. "I'm not going to beg, but I will make a speech tomorrow. Jesse is the only one I have to convince, I think. Sam will vote for me. Frank, no way."

"Just having family on the board makes it weird," Wyatt said. "After this you might want to change that."

"If I'm still around," she said.

Wyatt polished off his sandwich and said, "Let's get married. Today."

She stared at him, her sandwich halfway to her mouth. "What?"

"You told me once you didn't want a big wedding. Is that still true?"

Bella nodded, her sandwich still in front of her mouth.

"We could do it all before meeting with the insurance guy." He ate some potato salad. "All we need to get a license is our birth certificates. I checked."

"Mine is at the apartment," she said. Her heart raced at the thought of doing it so fast, since they'd been back together for such a little amount of time. But then she remembered being without him, the pain she'd felt, and the excitement of being with him again.

Had he changed? Would his wandering cock come between them again? She wasn't sure, but she was willing to take the chance to get her lover, her Dom, her Daddy in her life.

"Let's do it," she said.

"I brought my birth certificate with me just in case you agreed." Wyatt put his free hand on hers and squeezed. "Eat up, then, so we can get to the courthouse. I'll call Hawk and have him and Jessica meet us there so they can be witnesses, if that's okay with you."

"Fantastic," Bella said. She stuffed the last of her sandwich in her mouth and said, "Let's go," around the mouthful.

"Tonight we'll make vows to each other as Dom/sub, and Daddy/little," Wyatt said. "You want to write them? I know we've talked about it before, but I think it's important."

"I will," she said. "After meeting with the insurance agent."

"That works for me," Wyatt said. "Whatever you put in there is fine with me. In this part, you're in charge."

"I like to hear that," Bella said. She picked up another sandwich. "I'll eat this in the truck. Let's go."

Bella couldn't help but stare at the wide gold band on her left hand as she steadied herself against her desk and signed papers with her right. She had been surprised to find Landon at the meeting, with a folder of photos for Chris, the insurance agent.

She apologized for not waiting for Chris before cleaning up, but told him they had a business to run, and had to move ahead. He said he understood.

Now that Chris was gone, Bella wanted to use the time to write the private vows she and Wyatt would recite to each other tonight. They planned on staying at her apartment where they could be totally alone.

Right now, she stood behind her desk, with Frank on the other side. His phone rang and once he'd answered he turned his back on her. At the same time she got a text on hers. She smiled as she saw Sam's name with the words: *CONGRATULA-TIONS! I'm so happy for you both.*

Small town news spread fast, and she was sure someone at the courthouse had texted someone, who had texted someone, and it was now around to her family that she was Mrs. Wyatt Coleman.

She texted back her thanks and heard Frank say, "What?" He wheeled back around and grabbed her left hand. "Son of a…"

He disconnected the phone and said, "You didn't think to tell us you were getting married?"

"Why, so you can congratulate me out of one side of your mouth while you fire me out of the other? Fuck you, Frank. I'd like you to get the fuck out of my office now."

For a minute she thought he was going to say no. Instead he just nodded. "I'll see you tomorrow morning." As he left she heard him mumble, "I hope he can do something about that mouth of yours."

He was barely gone when Lily rushed in, waving her phone. "I can't believe it! Let me see, let me see." She waved her free hand at Bella, who held out her left hand.

"You had time to buy rings, but not tell me?" Lily asked.

"Wyatt bought the rings years ago," she said. Her heart had thudded uncontrollably when he'd pulled them out of his pocket. She'd figured he'd gotten rid of them years ago. She still remembered the day they'd bought them, some nine years ago. They'd gone to the jewelry shop to buy his mother a birthday present, and Bella had seen the rings, wide gold bands surrounded by small silver rings. They were identical, one for her, one for Wyatt. And now that they were on their fingers she'd never been so happy in her life.

"I sent Sissy to the store for a cake," Lily said, "For an impromptu celebration. You should call your *husband* and tell him to join us."

"I will," Bella said. She hadn't told Lily about tomorrow's meeting. She didn't want to worry her friend until it was all said and done. Right now she wanted to celebrate her marriage to the man she loved—the only man she'd ever loved.

Marrying Wyatt was the best decision of her life.

They were sitting opposite each other in the middle of her bed, their knees touching. Wyatt wore jeans, and nothing more. Bella had on a pair of baby doll pajamas she'd bought years ago, but hadn't worn since she and Wyatt had split.

She'd spent hours trying to write out words that would represent the Dom/sub part of their relationship and the Daddy/little part, and she'd failed miserably. She had blank sheets of paper sitting next to her, and a deep-seated fear on how to explain it to her new husband. He'd brought a meal from his brother, which had surprised her on one front—not that he'd brought food, but he'd brought lasagna, one of her favorite dishes.

They'd eaten, and held hands while they had, then changed and gone to bed, not for sex, but for the vows he wanted to say.

"I failed," she whispered. "I'm a wordsmith, but I couldn't find the words to say I wanted to submit to you in the bedroom, to let you lead me to places I've never been before. To take me to subspace, but it all sounded like I was being demanding, and not willing to be led. I'm sorry."

Wyatt was silent for a few moments before he said, "You didn't put yourself in my place?"

Bella shook her head.

"Let me tell you what I just heard you say." He brought her hand to his lips and kissed her palm. "You said you wanted to follow my lead in the bedroom. So I ask you, who's in charge, Bella?"

"You are, Master Wyatt," she replied.

"And what is your safe word?"

"Even after all these years she remembered the one she'd used, that showed part of her character. "Cheddar," she whispered.

149

"My cheese loving Bella," Wyatt said with a laugh.

"So that's what I heard from you," he said. "Let me tell you what I expect. I don't want you to fight my lead. You're a strong-willed woman, and sometimes you don't want to give up control. But you know it's good for you when you do.

I want you to promise me when you walk in the front door you're either submissive Bella, or Baby Bella."

Bella nodded. "As you wish, Daddy, or Master, just lead me."

"Tonight, I want my Baby Bella," he said. "As your Daddy, I want to teach you, lead you, and tonight, calm you for what is happening tomorrow. Your last week has been stressful, and I know ways to calm you down. Stay here."

He got up and went to the suitcase he'd brought with him when he arrived. After he'd rooted around for a moment he pulled out a wrapped package about the size of a shirt box. When he was back on the bed she said, "I don't have a wedding gift for you."

"This isn't a wedding gift," he said. "This is for my Baby Bella."

Not one to save the paper, Bella ripped the wrapping off the package and pulled off the top. Inside she found several coloring books, and crayons. There were also two packages of paper dolls.

"Oh, fun!" she exclaimed. "Do I get to pick which one to do first?"

"Of course," Wyatt said. "Let's turn on cartoons and you can play."

Bella started to punch out the two dolls, then turned to the pages of clothes that came with them. It had been years since she'd done this, and she was thrilled at the idea of sitting here with Wyatt.

He flipped through the channels and stopped on a western. Bella stretched out on her stomach, resting on her elbows.

She continued to punch out clothes while Wyatt stroked her hair.

"If this is how married life is going to be, I'm thrilled," she said. It was on the tip of her tongue to add that most people had sex on their wedding night, but she reminded herself the night was still young, and she'd made a vow to let Wyatt lead them in that direction.

Once she'd dressed two of her dolls, one in a pretty evening gown, the other in a business suit, she played out tomorrow's scene.

"You will do as I say," the business-suited doll said.

"I will do what is right," the evening-gowned doll answered.

Wyatt laughed. "The pretty doll is right," he said. "Always do what is right."

"What happens when they fire me?" Bella asked. "I'm sure Mom will kick me out of here."

"We'll live on the ranch until the depot is remodeled," he said. "At one point you told me you'd like to write books, mysteries, remember?"

"That was years ago," she said.

"Is there anything wrong with following a dream?" he asked.

"I'd pretty much forgotten about it," Bella said. She walked the evening-gowned doll across the bed. "Should I try?"

"That's up to you, my love," Wyatt said. "But I will support you in whatever you do."

"Maybe I could use the theft of the museum items for a plot." She giggled. "I need another doll to represent Abby."

"I want her to be the victim," he said with a laugh.

"I know you do." Bella couldn't help but laugh. "I'll work on that for you."

Wyatt's laughter made her smile.

"Well, time for bed," Wyatt said.

"We're in bed," Bella answered.

"I guess what I should have said is time for sex."

Bella giggled as he climbed on top of her and pushed her down onto the mattress. "Are you going to announce it all the time? That's something new for you."

"Never estimate what I'll do or won't do," Wyatt said.

She liked that idea. He sat down on her bottom and bounced. Bella tried not to laugh again, but it was hard. This was so perfect. Wyatt leaned over her body and kissed her neck. Seconds later he was pulling at her pjs, and as bare skin appeared he kissed it.

When she was naked he straddled her again. This time she was on her back, and he once again leaned over. This time he took one of her nipples into his mouth, sucking and nibbling until she was writhing under him. When his weight left her body he lightly tapped his hand against her thigh.

"On your tummy," he ordered.

Bella knew what this meant. The only time he took her from behind was when he took her ass. It was something she had to learn to enjoy, because Wyatt loved it. He'd told her once that giving up her ass was the most submissive thing a woman could do. The fact he planned to take her that way on their wedding night told her he was trying to exert his dominance over her.

He kissed her butt cheeks, then lightly nudged her legs apart. When he ran his fingers over her anus, Bella hissed. She hadn't noticed he'd coated his fingers with lubricant, but they were oily and made her feel better about being taken this way.

Wyatt worked his fingers in and out, while he stroked her back with his free hand. When he knelt between her legs, she felt herself tense, and he slapped her bottom. "You're undoing everything I just did," he said. "You know you need to relax."

He slapped her ass on one side, and then the other. Bella

wiggled her bottom and when he slapped her ass harder she hissed and said, "Ouch." He spanked her bottom again, and again, and again. She wasn't sure what effect he was looking for, but it relaxed her more than his fingers.

Wyatt must have noticed it, because he slapped her bottom over and over. Bella arched up to accept the spanking, but suddenly it was over, and his hard cock was pressed against her opening.

She hissed again when something oily ran over her anus. Wyatt pushed in, and Bella grasped the pillow under her head. He worked himself inside her slowly, methodically. It felt better tonight than it ever had before. When he was seated inside her he put his lips right next to her ear and whispered, "Do it."

While he worked himself in and out, Bella snaked her hand between the mattress and herself and found her clit. She stroked and pinched herself as Wyatt moved in and out of her ass. Pleasure started to build inside her, and it was as if it were a race to see who could finish first. Wyatt was moving faster, and faster, and she knew he would hold back as long as he could so she would come first.

She grabbed her clit and pinched as hard as possible. Wyatt thrust into her and the pressure from his thrust pushed her over the edge. She came, her body seizing up as her husband continued to ride her.

"Fuck me," Wyatt said and she knew he'd come right after her. He collapsed on top of her, the weight of his body producing a feeling of contentment.

"I love you," she said. "I'm so sorry we spent so long apart."

"Don't be sad for what we lost, be happy for what is to come," Wyatt said. "That needs to be the theme of our marriage."

"As you wish," she said. "That works perfectly for me."

Chapter 17

"**W**ake up, wake up."

Bella opened her eyes at the sound of Wyatt's voice. He stood at the end of the bed, his belt doubled up in his hand.

"What the fuck?" she asked, sleepily. She picked up her phone and glanced at the time: fifteen minutes after five.

"I have to get to work, and so do you," he said. Once again I've made sausage, but I wanted to wait to make toast until you were awake because there is not much nastier than cold toast. Plus the coffee is ready."

"And the belt?" she asked.

"I want to swat your bottom to give you something to think about during your meeting." He cracked the belt in the air. "You'll be thinking about your sore bottom instead of your mother being bitchy to you."

"That's a wonderful thought to wake up to," Bella said. "I may need the spanking more tonight after I've had a shitty day."

"This will keep you from having a crappy day," he said.

"Fuck that," Bella said. She sat up. "I'll just have extra coffee before the meeting."

"You know what I'm thinking? In addition to the spanking you need to eat soap." Wyatt cracked the belt again. "I keep threatening it, but we haven't done it yet."

"Fuck that, too," Bella said. "You say fuck as much as I do."

"With as much soap as you're going to eat, you'll be farting bubbles," Wyatt said. "Get up, and go to the bathroom."

"Fuck that."

He dropped the belt on the bed and lunged for her. Bella rolled to the other side, and he missed. Wyatt got up and stalked to the bathroom. He came back moments later with a bar of soap.

"Get over here," Wyatt said.

"Fuck that," Bella said.

"I won't tell you again," Wyatt said.

While she loved the tone of his voice, she didn't care for the idea of starting her day off with the taste of soap.

"Maybe you should go to the Ranch," she said. "I need to get cleaned up and go downstairs." She hopped off the bed and started to inch around it. Wyatt stayed where he was; she was certain she could run around him and out to the living room without being caught.

Before she'd taken very many steps, though, Wyatt said, "Didn't take long for you to break your vow, did it?"

"What?"

"Wasn't it just last night you said I was in charge, that you would obey?" Wyatt shook his head. "So sad you didn't mean a word of it."

"That's not true," she said.

"Then why are you trying to run from your punishment?" he asked.

"Because it's not punishment," she said. "So I have a potty

mouth. You knew that before you married me. Besides, you told me yesterday I shouldn't give in to my mother, but I'm supposed to give in to punishment I don't deserve?" When he didn't answer she continued, "How about we make a deal?"

"I'm listening," he said.

"We forget everything that happened before our marriage."

"We're talking about this morning," he said. "Your mouth, and you basically saying no to me with that mouth."

He was right, even though she hated to admit it. "One bite, please? That's all. And maybe we can figure out a different punishment for my potty mouth."

"One bite," Wyatt said. "And fifteen swats, which is five more than I was planning."

Bella nodded. He was right, she'd agreed to obey, and she did need to watch her mouth, as difficult as it would seem. Wyatt walked to where she stood, and Bella didn't move. He held out the bar of soap and she opened her mouth. She tried to take a small bite, but he pushed it into her mouth and she ended up taking a much larger bite than she'd expected.

"Give me your ass," he said.

She wanted to tell him she'd done that last night. Instead she bent over the end of the bed. It had been years since she'd been spanked with a belt, and she wasn't looking forward to it. Her hands shook and she grasped the bedding in an attempt to calm herself down.

Wyatt must have noticed, because he ran the belt over her bottom, the touch of it gentle instead of harsh. The first swat was soft, almost caress-like. Bella relaxed a little as he struck her bottom three more times, the force deepening with each swat. By the sixth one she groaned. Bella was sure she would feel this the rest of the day. Wyatt continued to whip her bottom, with slow, methodical swats. By the twelfth one tears stung her eyes, and by the time he got to the end, she sniffled as she'd tried, and failed, not to cry.

"It's been far too long since your last spanking," Wyatt said. "Stay where you're at."

Bella obeyed him because it hurt her ass to move. Her cheeks were on fire, but seconds later they started to cool as Wyatt rubbed lotion onto her flesh. The soothing motion made her moan. One thing she remembered from her time with Wyatt was his aftercare. He might inflict pain, but he made sure to take care of her afterwards.

When he'd coated her bottom, he lay down next to her and pulled her into his arms. "I love you," he said.

"And I you," she replied.

"Do you want me to go with you to the meeting?" he asked.

"No, I'll be fine, no matter what happens." She closed her eyes and leaned into his chest. "No matter what happens today I have you, and that's all I really need."

Bella was barely through the front door when Lily snapped her fingers and said, "Over here."

Standing in front of her friend's desk, Bella wasn't surprised when Lily said, "Your mother is in your office. She seems anxious. What's happening?"

Bella hadn't wanted to tell Lily until she had information that would have a true conclusion, but now that Lily was questioning her, it was time to tell the truth. "My brothers will be here, too. They want to can me."

"What?" Lily's mouth dropped open, then she shook her head. "If you go, I go."

"You need your job," Bella said. "It'll be fine."

"So you say." Lily narrowed her eyes. "Your mother can be a bitch."

Not many of her friends would say things like that directly to her. Instead of disagreeing, Bella just nodded. "Send the guys back when they get here."

"Okay," Lily said. "But I might give them a piece of my mind, first."

"Don't," Bella said. "I might be able to talk my way out of it. Hopefully."

"If you don't, then I'll let them have it," Lily said.

"And I'll let you," Bella said. She didn't want to go and talk to her mother without a buffer zone, but she wouldn't run from her either. Outside her office she took a deep breath to fortify herself before she walked in.

"Good morning, Mother," she said. "You're early. Come to berate me about something?"

"Maybe I came to congratulate you on your marriage," Bitsy said.

"Since you told Wyatt what you thought of him the last time we were together, I find that very doubtful."

"He won't be good to you," Bitsy said. "You'll have a very unhappy life with him."

"Thanks for your congratulations, and your words of wisdom, Mom." Bella went behind her desk. She had things that needed to be done, because even if they were going to fire her, she wasn't going to leave things undone. She booted up her new computer.

"What are you doing?" Bitsy asked.

"I'm going to pay bills," Bella said. "I still have a newspaper to run."

"Leave it for Frank," Bitsy said. "Lily can help him."

Bella snorted. "You have an answer for everything, Mother. You have everything planned against me. I didn't realize how little I meant to you."

"You're the one who betrayed your family," Bitsy said. "I told you to let the situation lie, but you had to keep at it. You've exposed your brother as a…"

"A thief?" Bella said. "And people will know you kept his ill-gotten gains all these years. You think taking me off the newspaper will keep that information silent, but I ask you, Mother, what's worse? An informed story from the newspaper, or town gossip? Because I can assure you, people are already talking about it, and the fact you're not reporting it—well that will make people think less of you."

"Here, here, sister," Sam said from the doorway. "Great speech."

Bella lifted her gaze to the doorway. All three of her brothers stood there.

"Let's get this over with," Bitsy said. "Bella, under the articles of incorporation for the newspaper, I've called for a vote to fire you from your position. I vote yes. I'm sure you're voting no, Bella, so that's one against one. Boys?"

"I'm going to vote no," Sam said.

"Not surprising," Bitsy said.

"Well let this surprise you," Jesse said. "I vote no, too."

Bitsy jerked her head toward the doorway. "What?"

Frank stepped forward. "The three of us are voting no."

Bella glanced at her mother, who was looking at her sons as if they had shot her.

"No, you are not," Bitsy said.

"We are," Frank said as he closed the door. "Further, I've written an article for the next edition about what happened the day of the theft, how I felt guilty about it and told Dad, and how he took the items and told me he'd take care of it. Did you talk him into hiding them? Did you steal the necklace because it was so beautiful and you couldn't bear to part with it?"

159

"Whom did you name as your accomplices?" Bella asked as Frank put the papers on her desk.

"Billy Travers and Mitch Miller." Frank shrugged. "They both live in Dallas now, and before you ask I talked to them. I've written their phone numbers on the paper so you can check it out, as I know you will want to do."

A knock at the door kept her from answering. Frank pulled it open, and Wyatt walked inside.

"This is a family meeting," Bitsy said.

"And he's family now," Sam said. "Don't worry, she won. She's still the editor and publisher."

"That's great news," Wyatt said. Bella watched as all three of her brothers shook her husband's hand.

"Welcome to the family," Frank said. He turned to Bella. "I'm sorry for how I treated you in this whole thing. I was being selfish. Forgive me?"

"Of course," Bella said. She winked at Wyatt. "I'm getting pretty good at that lately."

"I'm happy the two of you are back together," Frank said. He clapped Wyatt on the shoulder. "But I guarantee you, if you hurt her, I'll beat the crap out of you."

"And he'll have help," Sam said.

"Yes, he will," Jesse echoed.

"Understood," Wyatt said. "And I'm glad to hear it."

Bella looked at where her mother sat. She looked defeated, as if her world had just crashed down on her.

"I'm sorry, Mother," Bella said.

"Don't lie to me, just remember what I said. You won't be happy with him. A year from now you'll be filing for divorce. And don't come running to me for help." She got up and pushed past her sons. When she was gone, Bella turned to Wyatt, who winked at her.

"Don't worry, I won't let her words come true. I love you too much for that."

"And I love you, too," she said. "What are you doing here now, though?"

"I was worried," he said. "Sue me."

"Too much paperwork," she said. "Thank you for caring."

"Always." He kissed her forehead. "I'm glad you're still employed, because I've set up a meeting with Jake Fargo about remodeling the old depot, and we're going to need a lot of money for it."

"So I have to pay for it?" Bella asked with a laugh. "Not sure I like that idea."

"We pay for it together," Wyatt said. "We do everything together."

Bella looked over his shoulder to where her brothers stood. Sam and Jesse had smirks on their faces, and Frank looked sheepish.

"Go away," she said to the three of them. "This is personal."

"I give it more than a year," Jesse said. "I'm very happy for the both of you."

"We all are," Frank said. "I might have been an ass before, but I really am happy for you. Mom will come around."

"No she won't," Bella said. "She always hated that I wasn't a boy. She wanted to be the only girl in the family. But if she doesn't accept it, I'm okay with that. I have what I want to make me happy." She ran her hand along Wyatt's cheek. "I let him go once, and it won't happen again."

"And I'll never betray you again," Wyatt said. "Never again. A promise I make to you all."

He kissed her, and she settled into his arms, savoring the feel of him, the taste of him.

"Oh, get a room," Sam said.

Bella giggled. She definitely wanted to do just that.

Epilogue

One Year Later

Bella's Musings
By Bella Beaumont-Coleman
© The Bookman Gazette

Yes, there will be food, lots of it. Those of you wishing to see the reborn depot house, the open house will be from three to five Sunday. We don't want early, or late, viewers.

Wyatt and I are particularly happy with the kitchen, which is large, and fully equipped with machinery that neither of us knows how to use, but we are going to take classes to learn. There is also a beautiful nursery, but we would like to ask that people attending don't bring gifts. The nursery won't be used for another six months. That's right, dear readers, I am pregnant. It is too soon to know if it is a boy or girl, but to quote a phrase, Wyatt and I are just happy that things are moving along at a perfect pace, and the child is healthy.

Wyatt rattled the paper in his hand. "Have you told your mother you're pregnant? I realize the two of you are not friends anymore, but letting her find out about the baby by reading it in the newspaper seems—rude."

"Are you kidding me?" Bella stared at her husband. He was on their bed, his back resting against the headboard. It was a beautiful summer's day, and she had the door that led to the backyard open to let in the air they both loved.

They'd been living in their new home for almost a month now, and she was still getting used to the newness of it. They'd added a few rooms, including a hidden one behind the closet, which was where their dungeon lay. There was a space in there they'd set up as her 'little' spot, where she played with her paper dolls, colored, and sometimes just sat and watched TV with her Daddy. That spot would not be open to the public during the open house.

When they found out she was pregnant, they turned one of the spare bedrooms into a nursery, which to Bella was perfect. They still had two others where they could host visitors.

"How are you feeling today?" Wyatt asked.

"Absolutely perfect," she said. "My life is a dream come true. I live in a perfect house, with my perfect husband, and I'm going to have a perfect baby to complete the deal. We have land where we can ride and be outdoors. We have stables where we can teach our children to ride. I'm not sure what else I can ask for."

"How about some editing advice from your perfect husband? Take out all this stuff about square footage, and how we built the house. It's too much."

"Excuse me, but you're the cowboy and I'm the editor." She waved her finger in his direction. "Stay in your own lane."

"Are you arguing with me?"

"When haven't I?"

"I'm serious, Bella," Wyatt said. "You're going to lose your readers in this technical stuff."

"I think people will enjoy seeing it."

"The people who will enjoy seeing it will show up to the open house on Sunday," Wyatt said. "Take my advice and cut it."

"And if I don't?" She put her hands on her hips and glared at him. "Will I be standing in the corner?"

"For months," he said.

When she found out she was pregnant, they knew they were going to have to tone down some of their play. No spankings, no hard play. It was going to have to be a somewhat vanilla sex life for the next six months. But other punishments could work, even though he was sticking his nose into newspaper business. Still, she could live with that.

Bella smiled at him. "Bring it on."

The End

Melinda Barron

Melinda Barron loves to explore Egyptian tombs and temples, discover Mayan ruins, play in castle towers, and explore new cities and countries. She generally does it all from the comfort of her home by opening a book.

Melinda loves to lose herself between the pages of a book. The only thing she loves more is creating stories from the wonderful heroes and heroines that haunt her dreams and crowd her head. She believes love is for everyone, not just those who are a size 2. Her books are full of magic, suspense and love, in all sorts of shapes and sizes.

Mel currently lives in the Texas Panhandle with two cats and a file stuffed with new ideas to keep her typing fingers busy and your heart engaged.

Mel also writes as Maura McMann.

Visit her blog here:
http://barron-chronicles.blogspot.com

Don't miss these exciting titles by Melinda Barron and Blushing Books!

Rescue Ranch
Aurora's Cowboy Daddy
Jessica's Cowboy Daddy
Leslie's Cowboy Daddy
Bella's Cowboy Daddy

His Party Guest, Book 5
His Lady Brat, Book 6
The Rakes of Mayfair Collection

Anthologies
Daddy Dom Christmas
12 Naughty Days of Christmas 2020
Ghost Seekers
Unexpected Doms
Heart and Home, The MacAllister Brothers
Scary Spanks
Love of a Cowboy, Vol. II
Holiday Heat
Dominating His Valentine

Blushing Books

Blushing Books is the oldest eBook publisher on the web. We've been running websites that publish steamy romance and erotica since 1999, and we have been selling eBooks since 2003. We have free and promotional offerings that change weekly, so please do visit us at http://www.blushingbooks.com/free.

Blushing Books Newsletter

Please join the Blushing Books newsletter
to receive updates & special promotional offers.
You can also join by using your mobile phone:
Just text **BLUSHING** to 22828.

Every month, one new sign up via text messaging will receive
a $25.00 Amazon gift card, so sign up today!

www.ingramcontent.com/pod-product-compliance
Lightning Source LLC
Chambersburg PA
CBHW020642180626
46816CB00003B/1092